D0615233

DOWN TO BRASS TACKS

"An Injun massacre ain't no Sunday picnic," said Doc Entwhistle. "I myself have only seen but one and I never want to see another."

"Excepting it wasn't an Indian massacre," Slocum said.

The doc's eyebrows shot upward; his mouth formed a pursed 'O'. "Thought it was. Thought you said . . ."

"It was a massacre, all right. Only it was whites," Slocum said. "Somebody wanted it to look like an Indian attack."

"I see you're a man who knows the trail, mister."

"It doesn't take much to read sign that somebody's dumb enough to leave wrong."

"Like—?"

"Like shooting all those arrows into a dead horse, when anyone knows how short the tribes are on ammo and so wouldn't use up their arrows like that . . ."

OTHER BOOKS BY JAKE LOGAN

JAKE LOGAN

SLOCUM AND THE PLAINS MASSACRE

B

BERKLEY BOOKS, NEW YORK

SLOCUM AND THE PLAINS MASSACRE

A Berkley Book/published by arrangement with
the author

PRINTING HISTORY
Berkley edition/August 1989

All rights reserved.
Copyright © 1989 by The Berkley Publishing Group.
This book may not be reproduced in whole or in part,
by mimeograph or any other means, without permission.
For information address: The Berkley Publishing Group,
200 Madison Avenue, New York, N.Y. 10016

ISBN: 0-425-11693-X

A BERKLEY BOOK ® TM 757,375
Berkley Books are published by The Berkley Publishing Group
200 Madison Avenue, New York, N.Y. 10016.
The name "BERKLEY" and the "B" logo
are trademarks belonging to Berkley Publishing Corporation

PRINTED IN THE UNITED STATES OF AMERICA

10 9 8 7 6 5 4 3 2 1

1

Seen from the high tableland, there didn't appear to be much left of the wagon train except smoke, a dead horse, and what could only be the bodies of those who had dreamed of starting a new life in the West. Already one of the circling buzzards had landed, and now a second followed.

Slocum sat on his spotted pony and studied the scene through his field glasses. It was nothing new to him—nor, he thought sourly, to the buzzards. It was a complete rubout, though, to be sure, they could have taken some captives, who would probably still be alive.

Once again he studied the surrounding prairie and foothills. Since there was still some smoke coming from the fired Conestogas, he judged the attack to have taken place not very long ago. And there was always the possibility of the same band of marauders being about—or, for that matter, others.

He made one last sweep with the glasses and then slipped them back into their case. Within a half hour, staying close to a line of pine and spruce, he was on a level with the disaster. He didn't hurry. It was only the foolish man who took chances or was impatient at such a time. He knew better than most that a man on the trail was allowed but one mistake—his last.

As he got closer to the dead horse and the smoldering wagons, the smoke began to be sharp in his eyes and nose. He felt a new uneasiness. John Slocum was a man who listened closely to whatever he heard inside himself and he knew very well that he was still alive because of this characteristic.

Now he shifted in his saddle, his right hand close to his holstered Colt .44, as he squinted under the wide brim of his Stetson hat and felt the familiar sensation grow in him.

Dismounting, he ground-hitched his horse, who was getting spooked by the smoke, the heat, the carnage that lay all about. As Slocum saw some of the bodies, he wondered who had done it. What tribe? Or was it renegades? The tribes were supposed to be at peace, but these bodies had been mutilated. Hands had been cut off. A man's head lay beside his torn body. The dead horse had been shot heavily with arrows. Studying the feathers on the shafts, Slocum decided it was an Arapaho party. Other charred and butchered bodies bore testimony to both the viciousness and the thoroughness of the attackers.

He walked through the devastation, piecing the massacre together from the grisly evidence before him.

His spotted pony, though still spooky, had remained more or less where he had left him. And now once again, watching the spooky horse, Slocum felt that strangeness sweep through him, that awareness of something further to watch out for.

Yes, he decided as he stood looking down at the dead horse with all those arrows sticking out of him: it was there somehow, in that tableau. Why had they shot all those arrows into the horse? And even as the question was still forming in his thoughts, he knew the answer. And it was at that moment that his attention was caught by a movement at the far edge of the massacre site, near the stand of pine and spruce. Something had just emerged from the trees. Instinctively, Slocum's hand had swept to his holstered six-gun. But there was no need. It wasn't an Indian; it wasn't even a man or a woman.

It was a small boy. He couldn't have been more than seven or eight. His clothes were torn, his face was dirty, and maybe even bloody, though Slocum wasn't sure at that distance. He appeared not to see the man standing there by the arrowed horse. He was staring, and now as he came closer, Slocum saw that under that big crop of corn-yellow hair the boy's eyes were glazed, sightless. He was staring, but he was staring at something Slocum could not see. He realized then that the boy was either blind or was simply gripped by what he carried inside himself.

There was only the boy, there was nobody else—only the corpses of those who had been in the wagon train. Slocum had tried to get him to speak, but the boy didn't even try. It was a question whether he even heard Slocum. He simply continued to stare into space. What he saw there, Slocum could only imagine.

"You'll have to ride up behind me," he told the boy.

The boy said nothing, made no move toward the spotted horse.

"Get up there back of my saddle. You can hang on to me."

The boy remained motionless.

Slocum stepped into the stirrup and swung up into the stock saddle, while the horse took a step away from the boy. Slocum kicked him closer. Leaning down a little, he said, "Gimme your arm and climb up here back of me."

The boy still didn't move. He gave no indication at all that he might even have heard. Not once did he look at Slocum or in any way acknowledge his presence.

Slocum told him one more time, and when he still didn't move, he leaned down and slapped him right across the face. That didn't do it, and so he dismounted and, without any resistance on the boy's part, lifted him and tied him across his saddle skirt, behind the cantle, using rawhide pigging string and his lariat rope. He was beginning to be concerned that some of the attackers might take a notion to return.

Even so, he took another moment to look at the dead horse with the arrows sticking out of him. And then he realized what it was that had bothered him: the arrows had been shot into the animal after it was already dead.

The sun was halfway down the afternoon sky when they rode away from the massacre site. Something in Slocum wanted to bury the bodies, but he took the wiser course of getting away with the boy.

After they had gone a distance Slocum untied the boy and sat him on the horse, just behind him, and told him to hold on while they rode. When his new companion refused to put his arms around him to hold on, Slocum tied his wrists together, then looped the rope around his own waist.

At least he'd be sitting up and not lying face-down, he reasoned. But all his efforts to get the boy to talk brought nothing.

That night they made camp by a creek lined with willows. But the boy wouldn't eat. When Slocum lay down on his bedroll, he had one end of his lariat rope tied around the boy and the other end wrapped around his own left arm.

He slept lightly, watching the boy from time to time during the night. The lad simply sat on the blanket Slocum had given him, staring into the dark.

Stoneville, as one visitor had put it, was a town as raw as an open wound and as wild as an Indian attack. The town had two dozen saloons, a half-dozen gambling establishments, and sufficient fancy houses to keep both customers and patrons surfeited. Stoneville was said to be built on top of a mountain of silver and gold. It was the eternal horn of plenty, and the traveler who spent his last dollar for a bed in the Jersey Hotel could feel confident that he might be a millionaire in a few months; at the same time, as he would shortly learn in the days to come, he might just as easily and swiftly be dead.

The noise in Stoneville never let up. All night long the sound of hammering, chopping, the squeak of wagon wheels, the roar of the saloons, the shouting of men, and the sharp slapping of gunshots maintained a level of intensity that was unique even for the mining or cattle towns that dotted the West. Indeed, the local newspaper carefully reported the night's violence in a column aptly titled "Breakfast Bullets."

For a full year the newcomers were indeed a streaming torrent of flesh, noise, and violence. They came on foot, on horseback, by mule, in covered wagons, and in stagecoaches. Mississippi gamblers, farm boys, eastern businessmen, immigrants, dubious ladies with talent to burn, the young, the old, even the ancient came seeking one last chance.

Among this riot of humanity came those tight-lipped, frozen-eyed men who did no prospecting with pick and shovel, but who took their wealth in secondary fashion—not from the earth, but from their fellow man.

Things finally got so bad that a United States marshal was sent. His name was soon forgotten after he was cut down in a hail of bullets. A second lawman suffered the same fate, lasting only a day longer than his predecessor. A third man with a tin star on his shirt lasted longer. He lasted through a savage shooting spree in Harry Skull's Saloon and Entertainment Parlor, where he killed three toughs who were trying to take the place apart. And he lasted through a draw-and-shoot gunfight with one Cole McGonigle, a slick gunfighter with an established reputation. Cole's rep didn't do a thing for him when Marshal Clay Hardy drilled him plumb center between his hairy eyebrows. And Marshal Hardy outlasted the

Golinken twins, who were identical in appearance and in the speed and accuracy of their gunmanship. They were also identical in appearance and gunmanship as they lay in Kneecaps McFadden's carpenter shop—side by side on their backs—while Kneecaps, who was also the town coroner, measured them and built them a neat double coffin, using leftover lumber from the Jersey Hotel.

But the sparky little marshal with the gun arm swift as a striking snake, and equally accurate, didn't outlast the twins' brother, Miller Golinken, who was sensible enough to know his own limitations and so carefully drilled the marshal in the back, shooting from an alley in the dead of night.

By the time John Slocum and his young companion reached Stoneville, which was the nearest town, the latest marshal was already buried, and some weeks had passed with no word coming from Fort Fitzwilliam about a new lawman for the feisty town.

He discovered too that news of the massacre of the wagon train had already reached Stoneville, having first passed through Fort Fitzwilliam. But no one considered the town to be in any danger. The attack had taken place a long way off, in the northeastern part of the territory, at Moon Basin.

2

"Well, he don't speak, and that's for sure," Dr. Franklin Entwhistle announced following his examination of the boy.

"For Christ sake, Doc," snorted Slocum. "A blind man could've told that."

The doctor was unmoved. Years on the frontier had brought him a sour equanimity that neither barbs nor bombast nor even flattery could penetrate. Doc had seen the high and the low—about all of it. For an instant, though, he was tempted to tell the big man with the raven-black hair and bright green eyes to take the kid to a blind man just to make sure, but he held his tongue. The man who had brought the lad in to see him didn't look the type who cared for banter or the gratuitous acid comment.

"What I am saying," the doctor said patiently, "is that maybe he don't want to speak. Maybe he just don't have anything to say. And then again, maybe he's deaf."

"What'll I do, then?" Slocum asked.

"Give him time. Wait and see."

"Shit take it. I got to find someplace to leave him."

"Huh." Doc Entwhistle scratched his gray head. He was a medium-sized man, with a long, thin nose, big ears, and the beginning of wattles under his chin. His gray eyes were milky, giving the impression that he was miles away. But Doc, people said, was sharp as a tack. "Took you for the new marshal when you first walked in," he said now.

"I am not a lawman. Do you see me wearing any sign?"

"Nope. But then, around Stoneville a man of the law don't always wear tin. It ain't healthy to show off."

"I have to find a place for this boy here," Slocum said, looking plumb center at the doctor. "I figure you as a man who could help me."

"I'll ask about. Maybe you could try somebody like the Widow Hardy. She lives just at the end of town, before you hit the south trail."

He had tested the boy, and Slocum was satisfied that he knew his business, but he had come up with nothing helpful.

Now he repeated what he had said earlier. "You'll just have to wait. The boy has had the shit scared out of him. What the hell—a Injun massacre ain't no Sunday picnic. I myself have seen but one, and I never want to see another."

"Excepting it wasn't an Indian massacre," Slocum said.

The doc's eyebrows shot upward; his mouth formed a pursed 'O'. "Thought it was. Thought you said—"

"It was a massacre, all right. Only it was whites," Slocum said.

The doctor stared at him, one hand plunged into his waistband, the other in his hip pocket, scratching. "By golly, ain't that the one!"

"Somebody wanted it to look like an Indian attack."

"I see you're a man who knows the trail, mister."

"It doesn't take much to read sign that somebody's dumb enough to leave wrong."

"Like?"

"Like shooting all those arrows into a dead horse, when anyone knows how short the tribes are on ammo and so wouldn't use up their arrows like that."

The doctor sniffed at that, and offered his visitor a drink, which Slocum was glad to accept.

Meanwhile, the boy had remained silent. He sat in the chair where he had settled for the doctor's examination, his eyes almost closed.

"He has to be tired," Entwhistle observed as he and Slocum addressed their whiskey.

A slow whistle of satisfaction passed the doctor's pursed lips as he put down his tumbler. "I have heard it said that the doctor in this country is more given to the imbibing of strong waters than anything else. And it is true, Slocum. I assure you it is true." He was looking at the boy. "His case is not so bad. I think you're a man who knows what I mean."

Slocum said nothing; he was thinking of the wagon train.

"We should give the boy a name," Entwhistle said. "Or, let me say, you should. For he is yours."

"He ain't mine," Slocum said.

The doctor drew himself up to his full professional height, took a drink, and replaced his glass carefully on a table near him. Again, he drew himself into his role. "He is yours, my friend. There is no getting out of it."

"What about the Widow Hardy?" Slocum asked.

The doctor spread his hands, shrugging. "That's different. She might well take him. But meanwhile..."

Slocum had turned his head to look at the boy, and now found the pair of dark blue eyes regarding him gravely.

"I thought you said he was deaf, Doc."

"I have been known to make a mistake." Doc Entwhistle had a curious expression on his wrinkled face.

The two men were silent. The boy continued to stare at Slocum.

"I know he can't hear," Slocum said. "But he knows what's going on."

"The boy needs a name," Entwhistle said again.

Slocum grinned at the boy, whose expression did not change. "His name is Fidget," he said.

"Fidget?" said Doc. "That's a funny name. Why Fidget?"

Slocum still had his eyes on the boy, who was now looking out the window. "On account of he knows how not to," he said.

There was nothing small about Big Nose Hendry Google. The nickname was not uncommon in the country. A number of road agents, bandits, rustlers, and others of similar stripe wore the name proudly.

But Hendry's nose seemed even bigger than anybody's—it was thick, bulbous, and red. The rest of his huge face was covered by a mask of black whiskers. The nose stood out like a mountain peak surrounded by thick forest.

Big Nose Hendry wore gold earrings, weighed more than two hundred pounds, and was well over six feet tall. He towered above everyone in Stoneville. The miners and cowboys who visited the various drinking establishments and fun parlors somehow always seemed even smaller than they actually were in Hendry's presence.

But Big Nose Hendry was no miner or cowboy. Everyone knew his vocational bent—it was certainly not with pick and shovel, nor with a cow pony under him. In his hip pocket he kept a large bandanna which had nothing to do with blowing his big nose. It was solely to cover his beard, nose, and earrings when he indulged in his prime enterprise, which was holding up the stage, lonely travelers, or anyone else who might happen along. Big Nose Hendry was part of the Stoneville scene. He did some harm—like any road agent—but not a very great deal of harm.

On the afternoon that Slocum and his young companion Fidget happened into Harry Skull's Saloon and Entertainment Parlor Big Nose Hendry was enjoying conversation and liquor as he leaned against the big bar. From time to time he trumpeted a great roar of laughter, at one point slapping a companion on the back so hard he brought the man to his knees.

Slocum and Fidget had found a table at the side of the room, and Slocum had bought himself a whiskey, and the boy a sarsaparilla. "Drink it," he said, knowing now that the lad could hear.

He watched as Fidget took a taste, his face impassive. Then suddenly he accepted it and drank readily. Slocum grinned at him. "I guess any kind of drink will loosen a feller, wouldn't you say?"

Fidget said nothing, but he was really polishing off the sarsaparilla, still with no expression on his thin, pale face.

"We'll go see that widow when we're done here," Slocum said. "They don't have a marshal in this town, so I don't know who to tell about the massacre." He studied the boy. "I sure wish you could tell me what happened. Was it Indians?" he asked. He had already asked the question several times, and again the boy remained silent.

"Maybe the widow can get you to speak," he said thoughtfully.

Fidget said nothing.

The room was filled with its usual clientele, crowded with rough, tough individuals. Slocum had wanted to look the town over a bit. As he and the boy had walked down Main Street some heads had turned to look at them, and he remembered Doc Entwhistle's remark about taking him for a new marshal.

And strangely enough, at just that moment a man came up to the table where he and Fidget were seated and asked him exactly that. The man had been drinking heavily, Slocum realized immediately, otherwise he would never have breached western rules to ask a stranger his business. Then he saw that the man was one he had seen standing in the group around the big man with the big nose. And things fell into place. He could feel several eyes upon him now as he looked at his questioner.

"Who wants to know?"

The man who had asked grinned slyly. "The Lord!" He breathed the word, his eyes lighting up, boring into Slocum.

Slocum was aware that others had joined the group at the bar and were watching.

"You tell the Lord I am minding my own business, and He might do the same."

"That ain't a nice thing to say, mister. That's blasphemy! And right in front of that young boy!"

"And the Lord's name in your mouth is blasphemy. Now beat it. I told you I'm minding my own business. You can mind yours!"

Slocum didn't want the confrontation, and he regretted bringing the boy along. He had wanted to leave him with Doc Entwhistle, only he'd seen the doc was going out on a call. Well, it was the way it was. He waited. And then it came.

"We take real kindly to lawmen here in Stoneville," the man who had accosted him said. He was thin, wiry, and had a wart on the end of his long nose. But he was also suddenly wary as he saw the look that came into Slocum's eyes. Due to his apparent dosage of trail whiskey, the thin man hadn't been sharp enough to notice much of anything before this moment.

He was about to go on when a loud, brutish voice cut in. "We take kindly enough to lawmen to keep 'em here permanent, mister." It was Big Nose Hendry, and he followed his words with a great trumpeting laugh, which was taken up by his companions.

Slocum took a quick look at Fidget, who didn't seem at all alarmed. He'd surely witnessed much worse.

Now suddenly the man with the huge nose was standing right there in front of their table, having shoved the thin man aside—and almost off his feet.

"Where's your tin, lawman?" Big Nose asked the question with a little baby voice, squinting his eyes and wiggling his fingers at the man seated at the table with the boy. "I don't believe you to be a real, honest-to-goodness lawman till I see your badge, your tin"—and suddenly, with a tremendous roar—"and your yeller-belly guts!"

Slocum had been sitting in the usual saloon-type chair, a round-backed, heavy wooden piece of furniture which under certain circumstances proved itself a formidable weapon. As now.

In one fluid movement, Slocum was up on his feet, sidestepped, and whipped the chair around from behind him, shoving it in front of the giant Big Nose, who had started to charge until he fell into the chair. Slocum's smashing fist, landing behind Big Nose's ear, sounded all through the charged room. And so did the crash as the big man hit the floor, taking the chair with him. Slocum had put every ounce of himself into that punch, along with perfect timing. Big Nose Hendry Google was out.

"Jesus!" somebody muttered, cutting into the awe that had swept the room.

The thin man who had accosted Slocum looked in the direction of the voice. "Christ," he added.

"Anybody else want to make that mistake?" Slocum said.

He waited a moment in the ensuing silence, and then he said, "C'mon, Fidget." And he nodded at the boy, who had said nothing, nor had he moved or showed any expression on his face during the encounter.

Slocum turned on his heel, an opening appeared in the crowd, and with the boy following him he walked out of Harry Skull's Saloon and Entertainment Parlor.

In the street, the sun was burning down. People were moving as they had been when he and Fidget had entered the saloon. He knew he had to put the boy somewhere now, for there was going to be trouble, and it could be big trouble.

"How about something to eat?" Slocum said as they walked down the street. He looked down at the top of the yellow thatch of hair, but there was no response.

The rest of their journey was done in silence, while Slocum felt the eyes of a number of passersby regarding them. Maybe word had gotten out quickly about his confrontation with Big Nose Hendry Google. But no one said anything. The eyes, when Slocum confronted them, dropped quickly away.

He found the house of the Widow Hardy without any trouble. Doc Entwhistle's directions had been clear; and besides, Stoneville wasn't the kind of place a man could get lost in. The small frame house stood at the end of town, and as the man and boy approached, Slocum caught the glint of sunlight on the front windows. The house was obviously neat, clean, cared for. A small bed of flowers ran along the plot of land that served as a front yard, bordering the roadway. It was the last house before the roadway turned into a trail. And it seemed to stand alone, even though it was one of six houses that ran more or less in a line after Main Street and its boardwalk ended. For Slocum the Widow Hardy's house told something about the Widow Hardy. He expected she too would be neat, cared for, with a dignity that would be unassailable. He had met a number of such women in the West. They were tough, honest, and fair. But they could be difficult. He hoped that this would be a good choice for him to leave his charge. And he was surprised suddenly to see that he was more concerned about the boy than he had thought he was. But the moment passed out of his mind as he lifted the knocker and sounded their arrival.

It was a heavy brass knocker, the kind of thing, he supposed, that the family had brought with them from way back where they'd started from. And the widow was obviously now part of that pioneer tradition.

Meanwhile, as they waited, the boy still kept his silence. And the wait lengthened. Slocum was just about to reach for the knocker again when the door opened.

A lovely young woman stood there before them. She was of average height but beautifully proportioned in both face and figure. She had high cheekbones—a feature Slocum had always favored—dark brown hair, widely spaced eyes, and full lips. From long experience in the art of sizing up a member of the opposite sex, Slocum looked at her hands. They were small, neat, and to his practiced eye appeared to fit perfectly with the rest of her.

"Good day, sir."

She wasn't smiling, yet her whole demeanor gave off the quality of welcome. And Slocum had the feeling of a softness in her that was more so than in the average woman he had known. Her grace of movement as she opened the door a little wider was not lost on him.

"Uh . . . miss, we are looking for the Widow Hardy's house. Doc Entwhistle told us this one."

"This is the house." She was looking at the boy. And now she was smiling. Her large brown eyes were shining. And Slocum felt something stir inside him.

"Is the Widow Hardy at home?" he asked.

"I am the Widow Hardy."

Slocum's jaw dropped, and he swallowed quickly, while whatever it was that he had felt stirring inside of him now began to race.

Suddenly, he reached up and removed his hat. And instantly saw the faint smile that she stopped almost before it started.

"What is it you wish to see me about, sir?"

"My boy here. I mean, this boy."

They both turned to look at the boy, who was silently regarding them.

"Won't you come in? Forgive me."

In another moment they were seated in the parlor of the house.

"Sir, I didn't catch your name?" She was sitting forward in her armchair, attentive, yet, it seemed to Slocum, thoroughly at ease.

"Slocum, ma'am. I'm John Slocum. And this here—he is Fidget."

"Fidget? What a nice name." And she turned her full gaze on the boy, smiling as though it was the most natural thing in the world for her to meet a young boy named Fidget who just sat in his chair staring at her.

Slocum realized he wasn't doing much better himself.

"Fidget doesn't speak," he said.

"I realized that." Her tone was very matter-of-fact.

"I found him at an Indian massacre, back a good ride from here, close by the mountains."

"Well, was he alone?" She had not taken her eyes off the boy until she said those words, and now she turned her attention back to Slocum.

"He was the only one—man or animal—that was left." And he saw the pain come into her brown eyes.

"And he hasn't said anything since you found him?"

"That's the size of it. Doc Entwhistle gave us your name on account of I'm looking for someone to leave him with."

"I see." And her eyes widened. "Why do you want to leave him somewhere, Mr. Slocum?"

Slocum shrugged. "I would reckon that'd be easy enough to figure out, ma'am. I'm a trailsman. The boy needs more'n that."

"I see." Suddenly she got up and walked over to where the boy was sitting and squatted down with her forearms on her knees. Canting her head a little, she looked directly at him. "Fidget, would you like something to eat?"

He had been looking down at the floor, and now he raised his head, with his large blue eyes fully on her. His lips moved, just a little. But he stayed silent.

For an instant Slocum thought he might speak.

"I'll get you something I'm sure you'll like," the woman whom Doc Entwhistle had referred to as "the Widow Hardy" said.

Slocum followed her out to the kitchen. "I can give some money toward him," he said.

"I want more than that." She had turned abruptly to face him.

He noticed a freckle on her cheek. And he felt something pull at his chest. "What?"

"I will try it for a while, but I have a question."

"Ask it."

"Are you planning on staying in Stoneville, or at least nearby?"

"I dunno." He shifted his stance and then said, "Why do you ask that?"

"Because I want you to help take care of him too."

Nothing could have surprised him more than those words. And he must have shown it, for he saw her drop her eyes.

"I am serious," she said. "I don't mean for you to be with him all the time. I'll keep him here, for a while. But someone—you—has to look for his family, if he has any. And meanwhile, he needs a man as well as a woman."

She was standing with her back to the window, and the sunlight coming in shone on her dark hair.

"What is your name?" Slocum asked.

"Ann. People call me Annie."

"My name is John."

"You already told me that."

And then they both laughed. When they returned to the front room Fidget was standing at the window looking out.

"I found this letter on him," Slocum said, taking a folded envelope from his hip pocket and handing it to her. "It's written to somebody named Tom; it must be his father. And it looks like it's from somebody named Bill, or maybe Will. It's smudged; I can't tell. Anyhow, he wants Tom to come out."

"Yes, I see," she said, her eyes on the letter as she spoke. "It says 'the pickings are good out here, real good, so come on out with the family.' Do you think it's a relative or someone like that?" And she turned the letter over to examine it and looked at the envelope, which was so badly smeared that nothing was legible.

"That's blood," Slocum said.

"Yes." She looked up, handing him the letter.

Slocum turned toward the boy, who was still looking out the window and had his back to them. "Fidget, let me see your knife again."

The boy didn't answer, and Slocum walked over to him and put his hand on Fidget's shoulder. "Can I have your knife?" And he reached down to the boy's pocket and withdrew a knife wrapped in an old piece of leather.

Fidget turned, lifting his hand as though to protest, but then dropped it.

"This was the only other thing he had on him,"

Slocum said. "Plus a spent Spencer cartridge."

She was looking at him with a thoughtful expression on her face. "You're a gentle man, John Slocum."

"Sometimes."

"I saw the way you touched his shoulder."

Slocum said nothing.

"But I know too that you can be hard and tough. I want you to stay with him awhile. In the past day or two you've been the only thing for him, and it would be a pity if you also abandoned him, as—his parents?—did, and the whole wagon train."

Slocum said, "I asked Doc Entwhistle if he knew about anyone named Bill in Stoneville or hereabouts who might have been expecting some family or friend to be coming out to this part of the country. But he didn't."

"And there's no marshal here to ask," she said, and her voice was bleak. "You know, we lost our marshal. Funny, when you came to the door I thought you would be the new marshal. I'd heard we might be getting someone. There you were with a boy who was obviously lost, and you had a question in your eyes."

"You're very observant," Slocum said. "I mean, noticing the question part. But I sure am no lawman."

"But will you make inquiries?"

"I will."

"I'll keep Fidget here, then."

"You're alone here?"

Her face changed a little then. He thought it tightened. "Yes," she said. "I am alone. I am the *Widow*

Hardy. You see, the last marshal who was . . . here, and was . . . killed—he was my husband." And she turned away then, dropping her head. She had said the last words in a whisper.

Slocum said, "I'll see what I can find out about the boy."

She had her back to him, but he could see her shaking her head, though whether it was in sorrow for her husband or because of the orphaned boy he wouldn't have been able to say.

He walked over to the boy then and gave him back the knife. "Maybe you know how to whittle," he said. "Maybe tomorrow we can both of us do some whittling. Cottonwood's good for whittling."

The boy looked down at the knife that he was holding in his hand, and then he looked up at Slocum. But there was still nothing in his face to indicate what he might be thinking or feeling.

"I'll come by later," Slocum said, putting on his hat and nodding good-bye to Annie Hardy and Fidget.

He closed the front door behind him and stood looking down the street that led through Stoneville. He wondered if a new marshal was being sent. He wondered too at his being taken for a lawman, both by Annie Hardy and the customers in Harry Skull's saloon. And also by Doc Entwhistle. As a rule he didn't object to being taken for a lawman, except that in Stoneville it didn't seem to be such a great idea.

3

Back in his hotel room, Slocum again studied the bloodstained letter, but no new discovery came to light. And for a moment, as he lay on his bed mulling over the situation, he realized that he missed his small companion. But he also knew how glad he was that the boy was in such good hands, and that he had met that lovely creature whom Doc Entwhistle had so dully referred to as "the Widow Hardy."

His thoughts returned now to the Indian massacre at Moon Basin, which had been so badly faked. Why? And who had done it? He closed his eyes while his thoughts played back over his own trail up from the Panhandle with the Rocking Box herd of longhorns and especially the stampede and the attack at Blazer's Crossing. For some reason or other that particular scene when they were just south of Honeywell kept popping into his mind.

They had been attacked before—by Indians, and by outlaws looking for easy beef. Neither had gotten away with anything except a good bit of lead. But the attack at Blazer's Crossing had been different.

He had joined the herd south of the Red River, seeing it as a good way to get out of Texas without drawing attention to himself. And it was so. No one questioned him; no one would on a cattle drive when you were a man who could handle cows, horses and men and you kept your nose clean.

There were two thousand longhorns in the herd, and the drovers kept them in lines like marching soldiers, as was usual on such a drive. The cattle stretched in this double line for over a half mile, with the point men at the head of the herd. The swing riders were spaced at intervals on each side, keeping the longhorns in formation and nudging them along. Behind the herd came the drag men. Then came the remuda, or cavvy, as it was called in the northern territory—the fresh horses with the two wranglers. The chuck wagon and supplies, along with the men's bedding, took the rear.

The men composed a tough bunch, Slocum could right away see. They wore no chaps. Their trousers were heavy material that had long ago faded into no color. The ends were stuffed into heavy boots, similar to those used by the Confederate Army. Like their trousers, their shirts too were colorless, while their hats were a variety of sizes, shapes, including even some Army hats. Their beards were long and caked with dust; hair was uncut and uncombed. Each rider was hunched beneath a blanket that had been thrown over his head to keep the dust out of his eyes and mouth. Each had at least one Dragoon Colt six-shooter stuffed into his belt, along with a bowie knife; and each rider had a rifle in his saddle scabbard.

It was just after they'd reached Blazer's Crossing that they were hit. Slocum had been riding swing when he heard the crack of a rifle nearby; and then another, and another. The cloud of dust that had been accompanying the longhorns now broke into a thousand parts, forming again into a huge mass, an avalanche of roaring death for anyone in the way.

Slocum found himself riding next to Ridey Hostak, the foreman of the drive, who had slid into working with him like a greased wagon axle. Together they rode straight toward the center of the stampede. Slocum felt the dust burning his eyes, choking him, cutting his face like hundreds of tiny knives. His horse, a well-broken cutting horse, turned quickly when the leading longhorns were almost on top of them, slowing down its pace to keep only a jump ahead of the charging leaders, enabling Slocum to strike at the faces of the closest with the hard end of his lariat rope. He knew that Hostak was doing the same, though he didn't take time to look at him.

The blows of the two men caused the leaders to turn slightly, then change their course; and in another moment or two they had turned completely around and the other cattle followed, bringing the herd into a milling mass.

The other swing riders of the herd, who hadn't been able to get to the leaders, surrounded the cattle, and now kept them milling until, as suddenly as it had started, the stampede was over and the herd was grazing quietly, as though nothing had happened.

Slocum sat his spotted horse, keeping in position as he took out a quirly and lit it with a sulphur match. Ridey Hostak rode over then, but he didn't say anything, just nodded. Slocum could see the foreman was a good man who didn't waste his talk.

And it was just then that one of the drag men came pounding up to say that two riders had been shot up, though not bad. "Willie and T.L. both took lead," he said.

"Who was it?" Ridey Hostak wanted to know.

"Injuns. They run off some head."

"Sonsofbitches," said the foreman. "Where are Willie and T.L.?"

"Cook's got 'em under bandage and I reckon some trail medicine."

"Good enough."

"What Indians?" Slocum had asked the drag man.

"Dunno. They were dressed real funny."

"How so?"

"I mean, they had a lot of clothes on. Most Injuns I ever seen had mostly bare skin on 'em."

"Could be Comancheros," Slocum said, looking at Hostak.

"You mean that bunch that's whites making out like they're Injuns?" someone said at the foreman's elbow.

"I'll scout around for sign if you like," Slocum said to Hostak.

The foreman nodded. Slocum had been glad to see he was still a man who didn't waste his talk.

Now in his room in the grubby Jersey Hotel, Slocum lay flat on the cornhusk mattress and stared at the ceiling. What was it that kept bringing back that stampede on the cattle drive? Something that was also associated with the massacre where he'd found Fidget? But how could the two episodes be connected? For it did seem to him that there was a definite connection. One, a cattle stampede, with two shootings but no one killed; the other a massacre.

As he usually did in such situations where he was trying to piece things together that seemed totally unrelated, he simply relaxed, lay still, with his eyes either closed or open, but now viewing the ceiling of the room as he let his thoughts have their way.

He was trying to visualize the scene of the stampede, the quietening of the herd, and the resumption of the cattle drive. But why did he tie the stampede in with the massacre? Slowly, he followed himself through the whole drama of the stampede, trying to catch each moment, each scene, each thought and feeling. He'd had the same spotted horse in both instances, the same guns, mostly the same clothes. The one event a cattle drive, the other an immigrant train. Both, however, were headed north on the trail that pointed toward Oregon and the far Northwest. No, that was stretching it.

The immigrants might have been heading for Oregon, but not the longhorns. But what was the point or place or item that tied the two together? Or was he just diddling his thoughts?

Suddenly he sat upright on his bed, crossing his legs and reaching to his shirt pocket for a quirly. Indians! The dead horse with all those arrows at the massacre site, indicating that these were not Indians. And the arrows had been Arapaho. And the arrow he now remembered picking up after the cattle stampede had been Arapaho. Yes—that was what it was. The arrow. Because what the hell was an Arapaho arrow doing way down by Blazer's Crossing?

There being no lawman in Stoneville at the moment, Slocum decided to head for the local newspaper office. And here he met the owner, publisher, editor, and principal reporter and feature writer of the Stoneville *Quarrier*, Ulysses Gulbenkian.

Gulbenkian was a man in his later years, with a trimmed white beard, watery blue eyes through which red lines raced in all directions, heavily veined, freckled hands, and a strong penchant for strong waters. He also favored fine cigars and attractive ladies.

He greeted his visitor abruptly, and in fact, Slocum felt that his arrival at the *Quarrier* had simply been a minor interruption to the flow of talk that now raced out of the white-haired gentleman, and which appeared to have been going on before Slocum even came in.

"As you see, sir, we are a booming town, a town growing by leaps and bounds, stretching our muscles, flexing our minds as we create our way of life out here in the great, great West! Sir!" He held his forefinger on high, rigid as a spike getting ready to fix a railroad tie in its irrevocable place. "Sir, we are in our youth, and we are conquering! Soon the whole of this great continent will have succumbed to man's pursuit of the far horizon!" He paused, breathing deeply as he felt a stitch in his back.

"Sir! Today, as you see, as you cognize, sir! Today we are a town, a village, a hamlet—if you will—in the very raw. But we are the backbone, the sinew, the blood and the guts of this great empire that is a-building! And we shall win!" He shook his fist in the air, and suddenly was out of breath.

Slocum waited while he recovered, aided by a glass of dark brown fluid which, he realized as the old man expelled his breath, was whiskey.

"Well, who are you, sir? And how did you like all that? What I said. It is for my talk tonight at the Wolf Hall Dancing Emporium."

Slocum had just started to say who he was when the old man raced on. "Do you believe what I said?"

"You made it sound real believable," Slocum said cagily, for he had caught the glint in those watery blue, red-veined eyes.

"You're saying it's bullshit, aren't you!"

"I do believe it's you who are saying that, mister."

A chuckle began to rumble out of the other man's throat. He fell again to wheezing, reaching for his glass and downing a solid swig, only to provoke a severe attack of coughing.

At length he drew himself up, calm for a moment. And then in a new voice he said, "I am Ulysses De-Witt Gulbenkian, editor, chief reporter, and, uh, chief culprit on the Stoneville *Quarrier*. As you must know, I have been asked to address a large gathering at the famous Dancing Emporium named after Charles Wolf, who one year ago tonight gave his life defending the questionable virtue of one of his charges—she hustled for him—who fell afoul of a delightfully colorful character named Reuben the Terrible. Reuben, after killing Charles with a sawed-off shotgun, took off and has not been seen or heard of since."

But then, to Slocum's astonishment, the old man stopped abruptly, sat down, and fell silent.

Slocum waited a moment or two and then told Gulbenkian how he had come upon the wagon train wipeout, had found the boy, and was now trying to locate a man named Bill.

Gulbenkian's wrinkles suddenly took over his whole face—he looked like a washboard—as he fell into deep thought, or at least appeared to.

"That shouldn't be at all difficult, sir. I hazard the guess that we could find such a person pronto, as they say south of the border. Indeed!" His face suddenly sprang open, the wrinkles vanishing. "A man named Bill! An unusual name! Indeed, I daresay I can in fact walk out of the office here and accost the first grown man we meet—grown physically, that is to say, if not mentally and so on—and I'd be almost willing to bet a small bundle he'd answer to the name of Bill. My good man, Bill is there for the finding!" And his open, offering hand swept toward the door of the small, cluttered office.

Slocum couldn't contain himself and burst into a roar of laughter.

"I shall use this for my column, sir. But—hold hard a moment!" And his eyes pierced his visitor. "Don't tell me you are the new marshal! There was rumor that someone had been sent. Praise be to God, we are delivered, amen! Except, you'll probably wind up in "Breakfast Bullets"—that's my column —the same as all the others. Well, have a drink here, while you're still of the quick and not yet the dead!" He reached for the bottle, missed, and almost knocked it over. But—and his speed, Slocum noted, was incredible—he leapt to the rescue, catching the bottle before it hit the floor and without losing one drop.

"I used to be quite an artful dodger in my younger years, sir. As you can see in the recent demonstration."

"I am not the new lawman," Slocum said. And he went on to tell how he had ridden north with a Texas herd and then left the drive near their destination.

"And you headed west then, if I know my geography, Mr., uh . . ."

"Slocum. John Slocum."

The eyebrows shot up to the hairline, the eyes sprang open, the mouth formed an "O". Slocum thought he looked like a rooster as he nodded, his bushy old head way up high at the very top of his neck. "Slocum! I have heard of you. Good things, let me quickly say. Good things! But I must say I'm sorry you are not the new minister of the law. I feel certain that we could all sleep better at night were you to take over that office. Uh, would you be interested, Slocum?"

"No, I would not. But do you think you can help me locate this boy's relative, or friend of his father's or whatever?"

"I can put a notice in the *Quarrier*."

"That would be good."

"There would be a small charge, Mr. Slocum."

Slocum grinned appreciatively. "How about donating it to a good cause, Mr. Gulbenkian? A boy, lost, homeless. The newspaper comes to his rescue. And so on. You've got a story going there."

"Indeed, I have always supported the needy, supported my fellow human, so to say, but there is a point that needs to be taken, and that is, I have no wish to weaken my fellow man by his realization that he can always count on my assistance. This in fact would weaken the race, and we would shortly all succumb to the savage hordes."

"Holy Moses," muttered Slocum in wonderment.

"It has nothing to do with Moses, sir. It has to do with the vast horde of ignorance that lies in wait for the unwary. Mankind has struggled up from the primordial slime century after century, and it is this great struggle that must be supported." He paused, took out a huge red bandanna from inside his coat, and wiped his forehead. "More from my speech," he said. "More bullshit." His mouth opened to release a wet chuckle. "I'm not in top form today, Slocum. Overindulged last night in the tasty waters. Fact, I got me one of them headaches that's built for a hoss," he concluded, lapsing into the vernacular of the open range and the trail-town saloon.

"Tell me why so many lawmen get shot up in this town," Slocum said. "And why everybody takes me for a lawman. I mean a lawman that's been sent special."

"It's mostly since the mines gave out, the lawlessness," Gulbenkian said. "The damn fools, they're just asking for the Army to come in and take over. Or maybe a whole cadre of lawmen. Slocum, you look like a man who can handle a gun, and mostly a man who can handle himself, and that's what they see."

"What I'm getting at is, are they looking to be happy or sad? Do they want the law in this town or not?"

"You are speaking of the general tenor of the town, the feeling, sir." Gulbenkian had returned to his editorial tone.

Slocum nodded, leaning back in his chair and crossing his right ankle over his left knee.

"Some people, the sane ones—more or less sane —want the law. And in one sense the business folk want it, though they also want the fast money. See, we sort of lost a lot of people when the mines closed, but now with the cattle things are livening up." His upright forefinger stabbed the air again. "Stoneville has come back! Never thought of it, by jingo, but you could be one of them slickers come to fill your pockets."

"I could be," Slocum said agreeably. "I could be."

"Except you ain't."

"Shucks." And Slocum let the sly grin spread slowly over his whole face. He could see that Ulysses Gulbenkian didn't appreciate being put down. But it had been necessary.

The short silence that followed was broken by the sound of the great editor vigorously sucking his teeth.

"I take it, then, there's no law in Stoneville. Is there a mayor, something like a council?" Slocum asked.

"There's a mayor and there is a council, but they ain't worth a pocketful of cold piss," Ulysses said. "I reckon you'll be finding out the way of it here soon enough, so I'd just as soon tell you now. There ain't no law, and there is not much government, if that is the right word. I mean, the mayor and his council are simply run by the English."

"The English?"

"The Liverpool Cattle and Sheep Company." Ulysses reached into his mouth with his little finger and, using his nail, adroitly managed to extricate a piece of food or tobacco, or whatever it was, from between his teeth. Slocum realized it was this that had caused the strenuous sucking.

"Cattle *and* Sheep, eh?" Slocum studied the newspaperman closely, but knew he couldn't force his pace. Gulbenkian clearly was a born teller of tales, and nothing would ever affect his tempo.

"Yessir! Cattle and Sheep—and whatever else they can lay their hands on."

"You mean they're into the whole town."

"The whole country. They have got beef and lamb, the cows and the woolies. God knows how much. And they own part of the railroad, and the water rights all over to hell and back. They are greed run hog-wild."

"You're saying they want more."

"And more! And ever more!"

"Is it the Liverpool outfit that's behind the lawmen killings?" Slocum asked. "Are they stalling on getting a new lawman for the area?"

"You see that broken press in yonder corner of this here editorial office?"

Slocum followed the direction of his host's nod and made out the press that had obviously been smashed.

"Liverpool?"

"Liverpool. Luckily I have a second press, though smaller and not as efficient. Still, it works. As long as there is life and breath in this aged body, and the will to nail those swine to the nearest tree. I mean, nail 'em with bullets!" He paused, cleared his nasal passages with a loud hawking sound, then spat with vigor and true aim at the empty coal bucket by the cold stove in the center of the room. "It is a losing battle, Slocum, but I fight on!"

They were silent again, and after a while Slocum began to tell the newspaperman about the herd he'd ridden north with, the Rocking Box longhorns, and the attack and stampede at Blazer's Crossing.

"I keep thinking there was something more to it than just a bunch of Indians trying to grab some beef. Besides, I'm pretty damn sure they weren't Indians."

"And that massacre where you found the boy— you tell me they weren't Injuns either, but making out like they were, in both cases?" Ulysses popped his tongue hard against the inside of his cheek, pushing his face out like he had a ball in his mouth, and he opened his eyes wide.

"Seems there could be some kind of a connection, is how I have been looking at it," Slocum said.

"I have caught your drift. And I am thinking the same, similar thoughts." And Gulbenkian nodded his big white head of hair.

"Then," said Slocum, "if there is a true connection it means that someone is trying to discourage certain parties from being here, from coming to Stoneville and this part of the country."

"Your reasoning is clear and irrefutable," Ulysses said. "Anyone would be a fool not to agree, sir!" And leaning forward, he slapped his thigh. A little too hard, as it happened, for Slocum caught the wince that came into his lined face.

"Thing is," Gulbenkian continued, "thing is, there's a fortune in just running cattle and sheep. Playing both sides is the way the Liverpool outfit does it. If you follow me."

"I do follow you," Slocum said emphatically. "But is the gold really played out? I mean, totally finished?"

"Oh, there is some mining," Ulysses Gulbenkian said, in an allowing tone of voice. "But the bonanza days are over and won't be back. It's taken folks a long time to realize that the big dream is finished. And now, coming out of it, what do we discover? Cattle and sheep! But we discover that Liverpool is already there ahead of us. With the range sewed up, plus the shipping—all tighter than a bull's ass in fly time."

"Tell me exactly who or what Liverpool is," Slocum said.

"Liverpool, my friend, as far as we are concerned here in this part of the country, is Sir Cecil Broadhurst."

"Huh." Slocum shifted in his seat, taking that in. And then he said, "Do I hear in your voice the notion that Sir Cecil could be behind the attacks on some of the cattle drives I've been hearing about? In fact, maybe the drive I came up with," Slocum added thoughtfully. "Trying to discourage some cases, and with others demanding a fee to get through."

"Sir, you have hit the nail precisely!"

"So Liverpool will have control, right? Boy, the boys are greedy!"

After a pause Gulbenkian spoke, his words loaded. "You will note that I am being considerably open with you, Mr. Slocum, until a few moments ago a stranger to myself, to this town. I have been open, baring my—our—secrets, if you will. Shall I tell you why?"

"I know why," Slocum said.

"Why?" Gulbenkian asked.

"Why, because you want something from me. That's obvious. Why else?" And he grinned mischievously at the older man, who, to his surprise, colored appreciably.

"Ya got me," Gulbenkian said with a droll little chuckle. "I will help you find the boy's family, Slocum. I have connections most people don't have. The newspaper."

"What is it you're after, Gulbenkian?"

"I am after the Liverpool Cattle and Sheep Company, and if that means that sonofabitch Cecil Broadhurst, then I am after him, or whoever else."

"Why?"

"Why? Shit, man, I don't intend to stand by and see this country out here ruined by a bunch of lousy foreigners with their fucking fawncy pawnts accents!"

"That is bullshit. I want to know your real reason."

"That is my real reason, damn it! But . . ." He held up his hand to stave off any further objection, working his lips swiftly, trying to find the right words.

"I—I do have another reason. A more personal reason. And it is as follows." He stopped, cleared his throat, and spat again at the coal bucket. With accuracy. Slocum had to admit the man was neat.

"I am not a young man, Slocum, but I do have

some good years left, some vigorous years. Or, let me say I did have. And, anyway..." And he waved his hands in front of his face as though erasing a blackboard. "Anyway, I had... have a friend, a, uh, here..." And he pulled out his big red bandanna and blew his nose. When he returned it to his pocket Slocum could see that his eyes were shining.

"My friend—my friend lived out at Little Neck Creek with her father, who ran about two hundred and fifty some head of cattle. Tom Spofford's herd happened to be in the way of the Liverpool Company. One of their herds, the Lazy Diamond, run publicly by Cal Bowker and his sons, happened to want a shorter trail to the mountain where they moved their cattle for grazing in the summer. Tom Spofford's outfit happened to be in their way. And, like I am saying, it all 'just happened.'"

"They run 'em through his outfit, your friend's father's outfit." Slocum spoke slowly, watching the emotion working in the other man's face.

"They not only ran them goddamn cows through Tom's outfit, but right over Tom."

"And your friend?"

"Kitty was ready to kill 'em all, and by God would have if I hadn't stopped her. Me and Clay Hardy, our last lawman. Clay got the boys who actually whipsawed the drive that wiped out the Spofford spread. Got the sonsofbitches, and that took some off of Kit and myself. But I am for sure going to even it with plus, Slocum. With lots of plus. Not with guns, mind you—I am not a gunman. But where it really hurts. In Cecil sonofabitch Broadhurst's pocket. With this!" He opened his hands to indicate the room where he put out the Stoneville *Quarrier*. "With this. The printed word. The most powerful thing there is, my friend."

"You are making yourself one hell of an easy target, Mr. Gulbenkian."

"That might be the only way I can do it."

"What are you doing about getting the law here? That's what would help you. Not getting yourself and maybe even your girlfriend shot up."

"I have just been doing something about it." And he held his eyes as level as a rifle barrel on Slocum. "I am seventy now, Slocum. I got the rest of my life as free time, is the way I look at it."

"I told you no. I am no lawman."

"I am not looking for a lawman. The town needs someone more than a lawman. We need a regulator, like those stock detective types. I mean—we need John Slocum."

"Sorry. I'd like to help you, but it just ain't my line of work. Besides, I would give you some advice. Why not take care of your friend? You start a fire going and they won't think twice about hitting your friend."

"I know that. Kit knows that. We've talked it over. Fact, it is herself who is more for it than me even."

"Where is she now?" Slocum asked. "Kit."

"She's staying at my place."

"In town?"

Gulbenkian nodded.

Slocum got to his feet. "I'll appreciate anything you can do to help me find that boy's family, or even friends of his family."

There was a funny look in Gulbenkian's eye as he nodded.

Slocum said, "Sorry I can't pick up on your offer, but I'll pay you for any expense in helping me find the boy's people."

Now there was a cold, determined grin on Gulbenkian's face as, still seated, he looked up at Slocum, who had moved toward the door of the office. "You know, I hadn't figured you hadn't picked up on my offer, Slocum. Fact, I figured you had, but maybe I had better spell it out."

Slocum knew then what was coming.

"When I first spotted you in town, a bell rang inside me, and on account of I have a wire connection with Cheyenne and other points of civilization —like Fort Worth, for instance—I sent a wire down the line."

"You believe in blackmail, then, even though you don't favor the methods of the Liverpool outfit."

"I believe in the ends justifying the means, my friend. But only when it actually does justify the means. I believe this is one of those rare times."

"The answer is still no. By the time you rustle up some law to cut my trail, I'll be long gone."

"You could be," Gulbenkian said. "But I wonder. You wouldn't be able to move fast with that boy."

"I'll be leaving him here."

He turned then and opened the door of the newspaper office and walked out.

4

The ornate barroom of Cornelius McTough's Saloon on Stoneville's Main Street was surprisingly deserted that evening. The mustachioed bartender with the big shoulders and hands stood at the end of the mahogany bar under a flickering gaslight and guarded the door leading to the cellar beneath the building. Occasionally a furtive customer hurried in, paid a couple of dollars to the man at the bar, and was allowed through the guarded door and down the steps to the darkened, smoke-filled, whiskey-smelling pit below.

That evening the match was between McTough's pug, a muscular barroom fighter named O'Roary, and the challenger, a big, tough cowboy named Honus Johnson. The spectators stood close together —it was not a large room—and in near-darkness, hardly penetrated by the gaslight near the ring, which was an affair with two ropes strung around four thick wooden posts. The boxing match was "illegal," and so the room was kept in semidarkness so that nobody would be able to see and identify anyone else. No one wanted to. Yet, while Stoneville was so often without a representative of the law, those who promoted the events beneath McTough's Saloon felt it the wiser policy to keep the fights as much as possible out of the public eye. Why ask for trouble when you could easily enough avoid it? That was the current justification for this seeming compliance with legality. Moreover, the goodwill of the more morally upright citizens was desirable when it didn't cost too much, as it was too in the case of cathouses and cribs. A further point was that the "illegality" added zest to the affair, and men such as McTough felt duty-bound to add this onto the price of admission.

The pugilists, stripped to the waist and splattered with blood, had been slamming at each other toe-to-toe with bruising results for more than half an hour. Mr. McTough noted with considerable unease that his man was almost sightless, with both eyes swollen from his adversary's blows, and he would certainly be knocked out shortly if the fight went on much longer. The salient fact was that McTough would then lose the prize money, which was not inconsiderable, to Johnson, the challenger.

It was at this point that John Slocum, in the company of Ulysses Gulbenkian, arrived on the scene. At the same moment McTough whispered a signal to a flunky who was on the stair. The message to the flunky, spurred by a sharp blow on his arm from McTough, brought the man's shout into everyone's ears. "The law! Beat it out the back!"

There followed an immediate wild scramble for the back door. Meanwhile, the two warriors maintained their feet on the ground, though just barely. And then O'Roary, McTough's bruiser, pitched to the floor. His opponent, Honus Johnson, staggered to the ring ropes, grabbed for support, missed, and fell over the ropes like a huge sack of wet washing.

It didn't take long for the evening to return to its normalcy upstairs in McTough's gritty saloon.

"I'm glad you decided to go along with my proposition, Slocum," Gulbenkian said. "And it is a pleasure, as well as a continuing education for myself, to show you the various activities of our fair town."

"Let's get one thing straight," Slocum said as they lowered their voices so as not to be heard at the bar. "I've agreed to help you out, but not officially. I'm not going to wear a badge. I'm target enough without a sign on my shirt."

"I go along with that, sir."

"And I'll run things my own way. If you have to refer to me at all, call me an investigator, something like that. I am not a sheriff, not a marshal, not a deputy, not a policeman; I'm not a bounty hunter. You got it? Maybe—yes—you can call me a reporter, a writer for your paper."

"I've got it!" Ulysses leaned back with his elbows on the bar as he faced the large room. It was now crowded with people, with the card tables filled, the dice games active, the wheel of fortune purring on the far wall, and the faro bank busy. From the next room came the strangled sounds of a sort of band playing the usual dance numbers, louder now as the doors were thrown open and some of the partners came into the bar.

Slocum had felt eyes on him ever since he'd walked in, and he was sure once again that he was being taken for the new marshal. Well, so be it. He wasn't going to explain it to everybody. Or, in fact, to anybody. He had made his decision to stay and take Gulbenkian's offer—or blackmail, to put it more bluntly. Nobody had to know why. And he really wasn't too sure himself. Except that when he had pictured again in his mind the boy standing at the site of the massacre he realized the decision had already been made.

He hadn't seen her approaching, probably because he was looking at a redhead across the room, but there she was suddenly at his side.

"I won't ask you if you're the new marshal," she said. Her eyes dropped to his shirt. "But do you wear your badge inside?"

"It doesn't tear my shirt that way," Slocum explained. "Only my skin."

She was sparkling with laughter, small, beautifully shaped, and with one of the most sensuous mouths he'd ever seen.

"I'm Lolly," she said. "What's your name? Don't tell me! I want to guess. John?"

"You win. Actually, my name's Henry, but I've just changed it to John."

"Slocum? Is that right? You look like a Slocum."

"If that's what you say I am, Mary, then that's what I am."

"I don't like 'Mary.' "

"How about Lolly? Can I call you that? Just a nickname for you and me."

"That's great." She smiled right into his eyes. "You know something? You're good at picking names."

"I'll bet you're a girl who's good at picking things too," Slocum said.

"Well, I kind of picked you."

"What else are you good at picking?"

"You tell me," she said.

"I'd say you were good at picking a place for you and me to lie down."

They laughed at that as they moved to a table and sat down. He had already ordered her a drink by nodding to the bartender, who now carried it over for her.

"I've got some bad news," she said, "but maybe you can help me out."

"I'll do my best."

"I just lost my job here."

"What do you mean? You're here, aren't you?"

"Yeah, but I don't have a room where I can take you. I'm sorry, I guess I sort of took advantage." She nodded toward the bartender. "They don't know about it yet."

"Why did you get let go?"

"I was trying to get some of the girls to come and work for me. So I can't blame anyone. I'd have got rid of me if I'd been the boss."

"Work for you?"

"Yeah. I want to get ahead in life, not always work on my back. See, I want to be a madam."

"I wish you luck," Slocum said, lifting his glass.

"I'm going to need it. But meanwhile . . ."

"Meanwhile, I'll be kind to you and let you share my bed with me at the Jersey Hotel. However, I don't pay for it. It's a habit I took at a very early age."

She was smiling at him as he rubbed his leg against hers. "I had no plan to ask you for money," she said. And she added, "Besides, I got to keep in practice."

"Lolly, I believe you'll go a long way." His eyes had dropped to her breasts, where he could see the hard nipples pointing through her silk gown.

"Do you like them, sir?"

"I dunno. I'd have to take a closer look before I answer that question." And he could feel his erection stretching his trouser leg madly.

"How about a closer feel, sir?"

"That too."

"And maybe a kiss?"

"I wouldn't think of a better way to get acquainted."

"I'm talking about kissing these."

"I'm talking about kissing those."

"Which one first, the left or the right?" she asked.

Slocum felt his breath coming in spurts as he watched her nipples pushing wildly at her dress, while her mouth opened and he saw the tip of her tongue moving just inside her lips.

"The left one," he said.

"Your left or mine?"

Slocum stood up, pushing back his chair. "If you don't get that thing over to my hotel room within the next five minutes, lady, you're going to get your hot little ass laid right in the middle of Main Street."

She giggled at that, following him quickly out of the saloon and into the hot street. Then suddenly she stopped.

"What's the matter? Change your mind?" he asked.

"I'd better get changed. I'll be real quick," she said, touching her silk gown.

"You rather I wait or meet you there?"

"I'll meet you there."

"Room six."

"See you in a minute."

"Make it less."

"Just don't start without me," she said.

Slocum promised he wouldn't.

"Thank God you saved it for me!" She let her legs fall away from him as she collapsed further into the mattress.

Slocum said nothing. He continued to lie on top of her, with her head cradled in his arm, and with his other hand under her buttocks, which he had been holding as they drove their way to the climax. Now he rolled off her and lay on his side facing her. They looked into each other's eyes.

"You're the man I been looking for, Mr. Slocum."

"I bet you tell that to everyone."

"Only the men, smart aleck."

"You mean, you like women too?"

"Not that way, for Christ sake!"

He chuckled. "You're sensitive to funning."

"I like you," she said.

"So do I."

"I like him especially," she said as she reached down and fondled his soft member.

It was soft only for a moment. As she began to play, it stirred into a thicker, firmer, and finally abso-

lutely rigid erection. She continued to stroke and
pump, and her own hips and buttocks began to
squirm about on the bed.

Now his hand slid down her belly to disappear in
her great blond bush, and his middle finger slipped
into her soaking slot. She spread her legs while he
probed deliciously, and at the same time her other
hand came across to take his balls and squeeze
gently.

"God, give it to me!"

Grabbing his cock with both hands now she pulled
him over on top of her, her legs opening wider as she
drew up her knees and he mounted her.

His first strokes were long and slow. He drew
himself out right to the tip of his club, then slid in
again, with maddening slowness, which they both
knew was all the more delicious.

"I want to be on top," she whispered.

He turned over on his back and then she was up
on her knees, guiding his cock into her as she sat
down on it, all the way to the hilt. And locked together they squirmed and thrust until neither could
stand it any more and together they came in a tidal
wave of come. It overflowed, and both felt it on their
thighs, as, still riding, they came more, and more
. . . and more.

He fell asleep under her, and only realized it when
he awakened with her breathing sleep into his ear.
Reaching down, he ran the palms of his hands over
her buttocks, then squeezed them.

Then he was on top of her, driving in deep and
high and with the utmost rigidity in his aroused
member, while she squealed and dug her nails into

his buttocks, his back, his shoulders, pumping in
perfect rhythm with his exhilarating demand until finally they came again, more fully even than before.

They lay exhausted, delirious with joy and satia-
tion. He slept again, and when he awakened this
time, she was already licking him between his legs.

It was evening, and the long sunlight stretched
soundlessly across the town. Slocum and Fidget were
seated in the doorway of the livery. Behind them a
horse stomped and nickered. The street before them
was almost deserted, for the livery was on the edge
of town. In the round horse corral two men had been
sacking a young horse preliminary to breaking him as
a saddle horse. But they had departed, and the year-
ling, a gray with freckles of brown and black, was
licking the salt block near the corral gate.

"Now then," Slocum was saying, "I figure it's
time for you to learn how to whittle with that knife
you got in your pocket there." He was holding a
piece of wood in one hand and his barlow knife in
the other. Slowly he began to cut into the stick.

"See, you can whittle like just doing nothing, just
cutting up some wood. Or, on the other side, you can
cut a figure out of the wood."

He looked over at his small friend, who was staring at him intently. He was wearing a cap Annie
Hardy had given him, and which was too big for
him. His blond hair spilled out all around it—like a
shock of wheat, Slocum was thinking.

"See, you can cut out an animal, or just some kind
of figure like a tree or something. Course, first you
got to have a real sharp knife. And you got to protect

your fingers and your hands or anything else of your person that might get in the way if you're not paying good attention. Let me see that knife of yours."

He held out his hand, and Fidget handed him his knife.

"Not very sharp," Slocum said. He picked up the stone that lay near his foot and began sharpening the blade. "It's when a knife is dull that you get an accident," he explained.

As he worked on the blade, Slocum could feel the boy's eyes on him. He checked the blade, sharpened some more, checked it again. At last, satisfied, he handed it back to Fidget, who held it in his hand and looked at it.

"You watch me now," Slocum said.

The boy's blue eyes were wide as he watched the man's hands moving with the barlow knife.

After a few moments Slocum said, "See, it ain't hard. Maybe I'll cut out a little wood tree. You watch me now. Then maybe you take a try at it."

Slocum could see now that there was a change in the boy. Something, some kind of softening. And there was something different in those dark blue eyes.

Then, without any warning, he saw the boy's lower lip begin to quiver. But Fidget remained absolutely silent as Slocum watched a single tear roll down his cheek.

Slocum looked away so that the boy could have his freedom. Fidget had lowered his head, pretending to be looking down at his knife and piece of wood. But when Slocum stole a quick look again he saw the tears shining in the evening sunlight as they slipped down his face. But not a sound.

There wasn't a sound between them as the two of them sat there, the man whittling his piece of wood, the boy watching. The sun was at the horizon now, and the rich light was moving away from the sky, the roofs of the small town, and finally from the two figures hunched in the doorway of the livery barn.

The square-shaped man with the high, shiny forehead, lumpy shoulders, and tight hips walked slowly across the room that was the office—rather, one of the many offices—of the Liverpool Cattle and Sheep Company. He walked with his upper body bent forward, his oval-shaped hands loosely clasped behind his buttocks. Sir Cecil Broadhurst was thinking.

When there came a knock at the door, he allowed an inarticulate sound to come barking from his throat, and continued to pace the floor of the office.

"Cecil, are you hungry? It's past time for dinner, but I didn't want to disturb you." The woman who entered was middle-aged, attractive in her riding habit, with her long blond hair done in a bun at the back of her head.

The square man stopped, facing her, and stood up, stretching his back. "Thank you, my dear, for remembering to call me Cecil. After all, it is still business hours."

"Don't be nasty, Seal, or next time I might not remember."

He grinned at her. He had a wide, very white face, almost pallid, with prominent eyeteeth that when he grinned gave him a malicious look. Sir

Cecil—the "Sir" was gratuitous—was proud of his malicious grin. He practiced it in front of a mirror not infrequently.

Now his eyes moved slowly over the woman standing in front of him. "I shall be traveling to Laramie in a day or two, my dear."

"On business, might I ask? I doubt it. Pleasure, yes?"

"Business, and possibly some relaxation as well. I most certainly need it. This work that I have taken on—in fact, have created—has been most taxing. Do you realize, my dear, how much money we're going to make?"

"You have given me an idea." She was smiling at him now, her eyes holding his.

He looked at her under lowered lids, and she thought how he knew how to make himself look ugly. Nevertheless, with riches in the offing, you could put up with a lot.

"I shall need you to handle certain things while I'm away."

"As always."

"As always," he said. "Remember, my dear, I trust you totally."

"Totally?" She grinned suddenly. "You mean, up to a point, you trust me."

He shrugged, flapped his soft hands, and moved toward her. "I wouldn't go at this particular moment, but I am needed. It's to be an important meeting." He had dropped his baiting tone of voice and was all seriousness.

Her expression too had changed. After so many years, each had found a way to manage the other.

This had been achieved mostly through the realization on both sides that the other was necessary. It was, therefore, a unique and almost wholly satisfying arrangement. Cecil Broadhurst—"Seal" to his paramour after business hours—had finally reached the pinnacle of his career—a lifetime devoted to the pursuit of other people's money. And Cynthia—formerly known as Angie—could rightfully share her longtime partner's glory. They had been through the mill together. Now, as "English nobility"—so fashionable in the Wild West—with accent, social manners, and the precise amount of arrogance, they had arrived. There was only one person who knew their true background—Archibald Holmes.

Archie also worked for the Liverpool organization, which was large. Indeed, Archie was actually English, while Cecil was only half. Archie presently made his headquarters in Cheyenne, but he had written Cecil that he would be paying him a visit shortly. The two had been partners for a number of years, and together they had worked out their latest adventure. Archie knew the Liverpool company and its workings like his own private mail. And moreover, as an occasional traveling snake oil merchant he had not only the perfect cover but was always closely in touch with the public, upon whom so much depended.

"Have you written Archie?" Cynthia asked now.

"You know I write him regularly, my dear," Cecil said with a slight impatience in his words.

"Can we have a drink? It is getting on, you know."

"A jolly good idea," Cecil said, and began to hum.

He moved to his desk and, leaning down, opened a small door and drew forth a bottle and two glasses.

"It's an excellent sherry, my dear."

"Then it's exactly what I need."

As he poured, he said, "Would you lock the door?"

She didn't answer, but walked swiftly to the door of the office and turned the key.

When they were seated, he held his glass high. "Let us toast our enterprise."

"All the way!"

Cecil Broadhurst sighed, allowing the warm liquid to circulate through his heavy body.

He was about to speak when Cynthia said, "Cecil —Seal—there's something on your mind. You'd better tell me."

He sighed once more, deeper this time. "It's this man—Slocum, he's called—who has just come to town. Perhaps you've heard of him."

"Slocum? Yes, the one who had a fight with one of the men in Harry Skull's place."

"That's the one."

"Somebody said they thought he might be the new lawman, sent from Laramie."

"He isn't wearing any badge. I have seen him, through the window here. He looks like a man to reckon with; that is, he carries a gun in a way that indicates he knows how to use it."

"But there are dozens of men about like that."

"Not quite. Not quite like that, my dear." And his eyes narrowed, his thick lips tightened.

"You know something about him?" She put down her glass and bent her attention more closely to him.

"I have heard of Slocum."

"Is he a lawman?"

"No. I am definite about that. Although I am having him looked into. When I say no, he isn't a lawman, it's based on what I'd heard already. And of course, that kind of gossip you can't count on. I'm having Dicer look into it."

"I don't see what the problem is. As I say, there are lots of gunmen in Stoneville, lots of toughs." And she made a face as she said the word "toughs."

"True. True. But you miss my point. You see, a lawman is a lot easier to handle, from our point of view, than an outlaw."

"I see," she said after a short moment of reflection. "You're saying, a man who's wearing a badge is limited by that."

"He is committed to follow the law."

"While an outlaw isn't."

"Precisely, my dear. A man such as I believe this man Slocum to be is free to do anything."

"And we—"

He cut her off. "We are not. We, uh, law-abiding folk must go by the rules. We are in this sense hamstrung."

A short silence fell. She watched the side of his face as he sat in his big chair, deep in thought. She saw his face clear suddenly. It was an imperceptible motion, but after a dozen years of close, even intimate contact with him she could read him.

She said, "I'm so glad you've reached whatever it is you're going to do about this person, Seal."

His smile was all over his face as he looked at her. "I've also reached another decision, my dear."

She looked at him, her eyes sparkling. "It's about time, for God's sake."

They both chuckled at that.

"But you knew when I asked you to lock the door."

"Of course!"

"The sofa?" he said, rising to his feet. And suddenly he was younger. His movement, his tone, everything about him was younger.

She didn't answer him. She had moved close and was looking into his eyes.

He started to undress her, and now she reached for his trousers and began to unbutton him.

In a moment she had his erection in her hand, while he had slipped her shoulder straps down beneath her dress and was fondling one of her breasts. There wasn't a sound in the room other than their quickened breathing.

Soon they were both naked and she had straddled his thick, rigid member.

"The sofa?" he said again, his voice a hoarse whisper as he squeezed her bare buttocks.

Cynthia was almost unable to stand. "The ceiling would be fine with me," she gasped.

5

And so he had not left the boy. And he had set himself up as a target for whoever it was who had it in for lawmen in Stoneville. Well, he would see what he could find out—if anything—about Fidget's family. And when that was settled he'd hit the trail. Meanwhile, he would have to watch everything really close.

He had asked the schoolmarm, the town council, such as it was, the preacher man who happened to be in Stoneville on his way to the next town on his circuit, the stage company, the people at the land office. And finally, he found himself at his last resort—the undertaker.

George "Kneecaps" McFadden, both coroner and carpenter, fiddler for some of the dances and the parade on the Fourth of July, was a man with a lot of lines in his bony face, a vinegar disposition, and bright baby-blue eyes. Slocum had no notion at all why or how Kneecaps had gained his nickname, and he also had no intention of asking. The fact was, no one in Stoneville knew, and that was the way Kneecaps, who was not so unlike John Slocum in this regard, liked to keep it. Both men favored the absence of unnecessary talk, both minded their own business, and both enjoyed the presence of Annie Hardy, who was Kneecaps' daughter.

"I dunno who this feller Bill could be," Kneecaps was saying as he stood inside the woodshed that was attached to his carpenter-coroner shop. "Could be anybody." He canted his gray head at Slocum, squinting with one eye, his jaws moving slowly around the chew he was savoring.

"Maybe it'll come to you," Slocum said.

"Mebbe." The old man spat at a lizard moving across the ground which was the floor of the shed, almost drowning it. "Give him a bath," he muttered. "Which I be needing for the matter of that." He sniffed, eyeing the lizard, who had recovered from the unexpected shower.

Slocum had turned to go, nodding to the old man.

"See you got yer boy at Annie's," Kneecaps said.

"Yeah. She's good for him."

"You figuring on leaving him there?"

"I don't know a better place." Slocum had turned back to the old man and stood stock-still, not moving.

Suddenly a grin spread across McFadden's face, and his blue eyes lighted up like he was twenty years younger.

"I was thinking of Annie when she was a button, like that boy, and her ma up and died, and there I was. And she was younger than that shaver there. Still nursin' when her ma left us, and the only kind of milk there was in me was trail whiskey."

Slocum broke out in a laugh at that. "You raised her on that, did you?"

"Nope. There happened to be a woman around could wet-nurse her. The both of us made it through, though me only just about."

The atmosphere in the shed had settled now, and Slocum could feel the old man was with him. "I'd appreciate your trying to recollect anything you can that might help me find whoever wrote that letter I showed you."

Kneecaps nodded, sniffing, looking out at the weather now. "Started to study it already when I first seen the boy over to Annie's. But I'll stick with it. Somethin' might come in. You never know." He was looking directly at Slocum now. "You aimin' to stay about awhile, are you?"

"Awhile."

"Some folks bin seeing you as the new marshal. I don't figure you for that myself."

"How so?" Slocum asked.

"First, I don't see no badge. Second, you got the look of a man who ain't coming, but leaving." He spat quickly at the hard ground. "No offense, mister."

"The name is Slocum."

"That's what I know." He squinted at Slocum in a slightly different way this time.

Slocum nodded, not saying anything. And as he walked away he was glad to find that Annie Hardy had a father like Kneecaps McFadden, but even more, that the old man with the vinegar look had a daughter like Annie.

* * *

"This here is good wood," Slocum was saying. "Cottonwood, see. You'll see."

They were sitting in the horse corral outside the livery. Slocum had given his horse a rubdown and worked over his saddle rigging. Then he'd checked the spotted pony's shoes, filing a place on the right front hoof, and inspected the frog on all four. It wasn't that the horse had really needed work on his feet so much as that Slocum believed in keeping close touch with him. As he worked he talked, and whistled low, just on his breath, always touching the horse and telling him in advance what he was going to do.

He'd just finished and straightened up when he saw the small shadow thrown by the boy as he came to the doorway.

Without a word Slocum got his barlow knife and a piece of wood and walked out to the corral. The boy followed, and now in the special silence that had developed between them each bent to his whittling.

After a while Slocum began to speak. "See, with the Indians, this tree has got a special use. The cottonwood. With the tribes, the Indians. Of course, everything is special with them—each animal, each plant, everything. It's like everything has got its own place, and is connected, related with everything else. Even each different kind of tree." He spoke without raising his eyes, bent on his whittling. "Like, now, with the chokecherry they make arrows, and they cut dogwoods to make tepee stakes. They cut pipe stems out of the ash tree. They make use of everything around them. You catching my drift?"

Fidget didn't speak and he didn't nod. Instead he raised his hand, signing "yes."

Slocum grinned. "Good enough, by golly. You're learning fast. See, all the tribes, they don't speak the same language any more than the whites all over the world. But one thing they all do know is signing. It beats the hell out of talking, for my money." He looked at the boy, lowering his knife and the piece of wood he was working on.

"This cottonwood now, it grows along the river bottoms. The Indians, they build lodges out of cottonwood. That's saying, the Mandan and the Pawnee used to. There's even food there in the cottonwood for the ponies during a hard winter. And guess what? They make a kind of candy cream from the inside bark. Tastes real good. I know you'd like it."

Slocum sat with his forearms on his knees, his hands hanging down, watching the boy carving. He had already cut himself a couple of times, though not badly. And he hadn't cried; Slocum took note of that. He hadn't cried, though it was clearly hurting in both instances.

"Here," Slocum said. And when Fidget looked up he formed an incomplete circle with his thumb and index finger, with the back of his hand up; then he extended his arm horizontally, pointing across his body to his left, raising his hand about a foot.

"Sunrise," he said. "Now watch here." And Slocum compressed his right hand so that all his fingers were tight together, with the thumb behind them, then pointed it downward over his heart, the palm in. "You do it."

The boy hesitated, and Slocum said nothing further. Then he did it. Slocum liked the way he had taken the moment to be sure, and hadn't rushed into a mistake.

"You'll make a good trailsman," he said.

Fidget said nothing.

"I'm so glad to see you teaching him," Annie said. "It's what I had been hoping."

Slocum put down his cup of coffee. "He's a good kid, and he learns fast. Maybe he learns faster for not being able to speak."

"A man could wish there was more like that," Kneecaps observed wryly.

"Now, Dad," his daughter started to say, but with Slocum bursting into laughter she was forced to follow suit.

They had finished supper, and Fidget had gone to bed. Now the three sat in the parlor of the Hardy house. Slocum was enjoying himself, first the company of the delightful Annie, but also the boy and the old man, whose sometimes acid remarks were notable. And while he was getting to know the girl, he was glad that at the same time he was finding out the flavor of the town.

"They don't trust you, Slocum," Kneecaps was saying. "You can tell 'em you ain't a lawman till you're blue in the face, but that don't convince them none. Law or not, the way you handled Big Nose Hendry told 'em you were not some circuit rider with a black book an' a lemon up your ring-a-ding-doo!"

"Mr. McFadden!" Annie's brown eyes were as big as moons.

The men rocked with laughter.

"You'll wake Fidget!" Annie cautioned, shushing them loudly.

Kneecaps fell into a fit of coughing, and reached to his glass of whiskey for support.

"I know what you're saying," Slocum said. "But it's like I told you—Gulbenkian kept asking me to help out."

"I don't trust that bird," Kneecaps said in a warning voice.

"Now, Dad." Annie shook her head at Slocum. "He's always telling me not to trust this one or that one."

"And I'm always right." He nodded his head in emphasis and dropped a wink at Slocum. "But you better watch that man. What's he up to? Why does he want you to push your weight?"

"He spoke of the Liverpool outfit. You know them?"

"Who don't? Sure I know them. They're gobbling up land quicker'n you can count what you got in your pants pocket."

"But, Dad, Mr. Gulbenkian has a right thought there, I mean in wanting the law." And she looked at Slocum.

"Everybody wants the law," her father said. "I want the law. You want the law. But nobody wants to support the law or pay for the law on account of you make yourself a target for those toughs."

"Any special toughs?" Slocum asked.

"The likes of Big Nose and his buddies. They spend their time in the saloons here in Stoneville, but their roost is out at Red Rock. Stoneville's like where they has their fling. Though I hear they've got a kind of roadhouse out near Red Rock too."

"And what do they do?" Slocum asked. "They pull some raids, then hide out. Then when it's cooled down they hit again? Is that it?"

"That's the size of it," said Kneecaps. "And nobody ever sees nothing, nobody can prove nothing. Nobody gives a damn."

"Except Mr Gulbenkian," cut in Annie.

"Mebbe. Mebbe," her father said, though with reluctance. "Mebbe he's thinking of the town, but then on the other hand, he more'n likely is lining his own pants pocket. That man for my money is a slicker." And he reached for his pipe and started cleaning out the old tobacco.

Quick as a flash his daughter had risen and, picking up a bowl that was handy, brought it to him. "Here, not all over my clean floor, please."

This brought a throaty chuckle from Kneecaps. "Tidy, just like your ma," he observed. And he grinned wickedly at Slocum. "You be careful what you don't get yerself into, young feller."

"Dad!" Her hands flew to her mouth in outrage and despair, as both men roared with laughter at the teasing. And John Slocum felt a warmth swimming through his loins.

Then the old man turned serious. "Likely, Gulbenkian's wanting you as a protection for his paper. He's written some pretty sassy stuff about the way things is run. And like just having you about, and looking to be on his side of things, he figgers will keep the boys off him. They busted up his press not too long ago. Hell, I will say the old bugger's got guts."

"I know," Slocum said. "But what about Fort Fitzwilliam? Will the Army send someone?"

"It ain't up to the Army, but the marshal business does come through there. The Army sort of has the office there at the post, but half the time there ain't anybody there."

"I understand that. Gulbenkian made it all clear. It really has to come through Laramie. But mostly it's up in the air."

"Nobody wants to take hold of what's a slippery business. You grab a rattler by the tail, next thing you know he's bit you." Kneecaps sniffed loudly as he loaded his pipe, tamping the tobacco in carefully. "Seems to me you got a choice to stay or git. If you stay you got trouble up to your eyeballs. If you git . . ." He let it hang, and in silence Slocum and the girl watched him finish loading his pipe.

"But you can stay and not take on as a law person," Annie said.

"No he can't." Kneecaps said it firmly. "The point is, what folks think. They *think* you're the law, you might as well be the law."

"I know that," Slocum said.

"I know you know it, but she don't."

The girl flushed. "Who is 'she'? The cat's mother?" she said sharply.

"That's just what yer ma used to say," observed her father with maddening superiority.

But it ended in a laugh. It ended with Annie walking Slocum to the door finally and saying goodnight.

He had started to turn away when she said suddenly, "Thank you for staying. I hope you won't go away. Not yet."

Slocum felt good about that.

All the time they had been discussing the lawlessness of the town, Slocum had watched the girl. He knew how hard it was for her, with her thoughts on her husband who had been drygulched. Yet he noted too that Kneecaps didn't slip around the subject. And he appreciated both the girl's courage and the man's forthrightness. But he knew now that, for the present, leaving Stoneville was out of the question.

Kneecaps had offered to walk him back to the Jersey Hotel, but Slocum had declined. Then the old man had cautioned him again not to go into any side streets or he would surely be ambushed. He was almost halfway to the Jersey when he decided something and turned toward McTough's Saloon.

Heads turned when he pushed his way through the swinging doors. Cornelius McTough himself was behind the bar serving drinks. And there was Big Nose Hendry Google standing at one end of the long mahogany with some of his pals.

"Well, lookey here, lookey who's here," sneered the huge man in the new silence that took over the saloon.

Slocum walked to the bar and ordered a beer. It was just the way he wanted it. It was the time to get something settled in this town.

He stood with his back to the bar, his left elbow leaning on it, his right hand ready for a cross draw. His eyes moved slowly over the crowd. There was a kind of shuffling, and Slocum saw some hands move toward their owner's guns.

Slocum's next words were loud, hard, and clear. "Boys, I doubt if any of you are going to live very long if you want to shoot it out with me. So keep your hands away from your guns and stay healthy."

He watched the hands move into the clear after he had said those words. And he saw the big grin on Big Nose Hendry's face.

"By golly, looks like we got us a lawman at last, don't it, boys?" And the chuckle became a roar of laughter. Then suddenly Big Nose stopped. His face took on an expression of innocence. "Sir," he said sweetly, "we will be good little folks. We will obey the law and do just as you tells us. Won't we, fellers?"

Silence.

"I said, Won't we, fellers?" The roar tore like a cannonball into the room.

The voices of assent swiftly followed.

Then Big Nose was sweet again. "See, Mr. John Slocum, we are just little old pussycats here. Just havin' a little bit of funnin'—and obeyin' *the law*!" He roared the last two words.

The room resumed its normal activity after that. Slocum sipped his beer but remained with his elbow on the bar, facing the room. He knew it wasn't over. He knew it was only beginning.

There was no gunplay. Nothing that looked suspicious, except to a person who knew the trick.

Now a tall dark man with a long scar down the side of his face walked in through a side door, his hands dangling at his sides. The dark man headed straight toward Slocum, and at that same moment Slocum saw another man coming through the same doorway and sidling off to the right side of the room so that he could get a good view of the bar and John Slocum leaning lightly against it.

Slocum was watching the dark-faced man striding toward him and at the same time was fully aware of every move of the man who had followed him into the room.

The dark man reached Slocum and walked on past him. When he was several steps beyond he stopped and leaned against the bar and said to Slocum, "So you be the new United States marshal."

Slocum was well ahead of the next step in the one-two ambush, which was for the victim, thrown off guard, to turn toward the man who had asked the question, thereby leaving his back open to the second man's gun.

The room was absolutely still. Someone must have moved, for a floorboard creaked. At that moment, Slocum, watching the dark-faced man, turned toward him, evidently in reply to his remark.

In that instant a gun roared, and to the astonishment of all, the man who had been standing against the far wall screamed with pain as he dropped his gun and gripped his trigger hand. Slocum had turned only halfway and, drawing with lightning speed, had fired his gun right across his own stomach. Before the sound of that gunshot had died, Slocum was covering the man with the dark face whose hand had swept toward his holstered weapon.

But there was a third party still to account for. In the next second Big Nose Hendry Google swept his gun from its holster, only to find himself looking into the barrel of Slocum's Colt .44.

"You can't get us both, Slocum," the dark-faced man said, his hand hovering over his holstered gun.

"You want me to show you how?"

"Whyn't you wear your tin, Slocum?" Big Nose demanded. "You afraid to wear it?"

"Both you men unbuckle. Right now!"

They did so, sneering, but offering no other resistance. The speed and accuracy of Slocum's shooting offered all the authority that was needed.

"Now turn around and get out of here. Next time either of you three mess with me I won't be so nice."

"Next time, Slocum, I'll kill you," Big Nose said.

"No you won't."

"You saying I won't, huh?"

"You won't on account of next time you'll already be dead."

And John Slocum's hard green eyes followed the three as they left the saloon.

It was early when he saddled the spotted horse and led him out of the livery. He had done it quietly, while it was still dark, before the hostler was about. He wanted all the advantage he could get. From now on, they were going to press him, he knew. And from now on he was going to have to be watching every step he took.

At sunrise he was well away from Stoneville, riding along the dusty hill trail with Handy Mountain, jagged and fierce-looking, looming before him. The place he was heading for was on the other side of the mountain, in wild and mostly inaccessible country.

Here, according to Kneecaps McFadden, lay a pecu-
liar formation of cliffs and canyons known as Red
Rock. This was the robbers' roost of the gang that
had been plaguing Stoneville and the outlying
ranches. Ulysses Gulbenkian had corroborated all
that Kneecaps had said about the situation, even add-
ing that it wouldn't surprise him to hear that the gang
was the same that had destroyed the wagon train at
Moon Basin, where Slocum had discovered Fidget.

As the rising sun came into full view, the narrow
mountain trail gave out and only dense, almost im-
passable underbrush of scrub oak faced Slocum and
his horse. Shortly, however, he reached a dry creek
bed that took him through the valley at the right of
the mountain. For some miles he made good time,
until the creek bed turned into a matted jungle of
scrub oak and blackjack.

Now the sun was burning down hard. It was time
for a rest. Luckily there was shade, though sparse.
He dismounted and loosened the cinch on his pony,
leaving the saddle on, however, and slipped the bit
out of its mouth so it could crop the short buffalo
grass more easily. He had extra canteen water and
gave the pony a drink, then took one himself.

Resting in the shade of a cottonwood, he took out
the letter again and studied it. He had shown it to
Gulbenkian and to Kneecaps McFadden, and of
course Annie had seen it, but none of them had been
able to make any more out of the smeared writing
than he'd been able to. And he was getting nowhere
at all going around asking for someone named Bill or
Will something-or-other.

He wasn't sure what good it was going to do him

now riding all this way out to where he might spot
the bandit gang's headquarters, except that if it came
down to a fight or a siege, he would know the lay of
the land in advance. He was pretty certain now that
he was within a short distance of Red Rock.

He decided to picket his horse and work his way
on foot up the steep trail that rose in front of him. It
took him nearly an hour to reach a wide ledge on the
side of a precipitous cliff. He found himself looking
across a narrow valley—almost a canyon—to an
even higher cliff on the far side. Fortunately he had
good cover, for he saw that below him in the center
of the valley were some cabins, corrals, a good many
horses, and men. It had to be Red Rock, the bandit
roost he'd heard about. And he realized that with its
inaccessibility, desolation, and lack of any obvious
trail, it was the perfect hideout—it even had lush
grass and a creek.

Slocum settled down to watch. He was in no
hurry, having decided that all he wanted for the moment was to see what sort of gang was here, how
they were situated, what were the trails in and out.

As the day drew on, more men appeared in the
valley. Pretty soon fires were lit, brightening the falling night. They were fires that would not be seen by
anyone outside the hideout.

Slocum had spotted the place where some of the
new riders had entered the camp, and before darkness fell, he hurried back down to his horse and rode
around the high promontory until he saw sign of
horses on a narrow trail which was evidently the one
used to enter the canyon. He still had a little light left
but decided it wasn't enough to look for any other

trail. He knew there had to be another way in and out of the canyon in case of emergency, but he also knew it would be even more hidden than the regular entry. He thought briefly of staying the night and exploring for the other trail in the morning, but he didn't want to take the risk. The gang would surely have outriders about. And so he turned the spotted pony back toward Stoneville.

6

"You see, gentlemen, this is the section that is so very important to Liverpool—to us!"

Cecil Broadhurst, in shirtsleeves but properly toileted—he was always a neat man—pointed to the map pinned to the wall of the Laramie office of the Liverpool Cattle and Sheep Company.

"It is a crude map, gentlemen, but you catch my drift. You get the point. This is just a part of the most important section that we need for grazing the herds. It is an absolutely key piece in our puzzle. I might say, *essential* piece. It is good, lush grama grass, and the cattle will fatten nicely before shipping east. But mostly"—and he held up his finger—"mostly it connects this section here"—and he pointed—"with this section here. That is why it is so important."

There were two other men present in the Laramie office of the Liverpool Cattle and Sheep Company.

The man with the huge mustache and very thick eyebrows and a Scottish accent now spoke up. "How far is this grazing land from Stoneville itself? And who owns it, or is it public? I mean is there anyone nesting there?" His name was Philo McIntosh.

"It is just north of the town," Cecil explained. "And there is one ranch, bordering Willow Creek. Here." He pointed with his index finger, and tapped the exact spot he was discussing. "This is a large rocky area, a failed homestead. Nothing of any use to us. And it would also look good to the public if we didn't buy it. The rest is open land."

"Nothing the Indians might, er, consider to be theirs?" asked the second man, a thin man with highly polished Wellington boots. His name was George Georges, the second name spelled with an "S." Over the years this had amused some people, but not for long. They swiftly discovered that George Georges was a man with no sense of humor plus the memory of an elephant and a talent for revenge that was famous. His companion, the Scotsman, was presently wishing the meeting would end so he could get a drink alone, away from George Georges. Philo McIntosh was also spending a good bit of his time trying to figure out a way not to have to return to Chicago in the company of George Georges. The trip out had bored him to the marrow of his bones, as he put it in a letter home to his wife.

"You are saying that we don't need to acquire that, uh, rocky section," said George Georges.

"We don't need it, and it would look better if we didn't."

Cecil was about to continue when the door of the office opened and a third man entered.

"So glad you've made yourselves at home, gentlemen, and I'm sorry I was delayed. One of the horses went lame." It was Henry Tillson, the resident representative of the Liverpool enterprise in Laramie. He walked quickly to his desk and sat down, slightly out of breath, a young man with a stern face and tight, narrow shoulders. He wore sideburns that seemed to take up the whole of his slender face.

Cecil quickly repeated what he had just explained to George Georges and McIntosh.

"And the operation for acquiring these lands— you've been working on your end I take it?" Tillson cocked his head at Cecil.

"Everything is going as planned," Cecil said, deliberately allowing a coldness into his voice. It was fatal if you let any of these birds think he had the upper hand. Ah, Cecil had dealt with this kind often enough to smell them out. The way they sat, the way they tilted their heads, the way they looked at you— the smart, smug sonsofbitches! Well, by God, he was within inches of having them by the balls. And then —then hear the screaming!

His smile was benign as he turned again to the group.

"Gentlemen, I foresee our plan going through without a hitch. And I want to say right here that without your cooperation, your support, your fertile ideas . . ." He opened his hands, bent his head with just the suggestion of sanctimony, wordless in his appreciation.

"I take it those herds we selected, the ones cooperating with us, have gotten through," George Georges said.

Cecil nodded.

"And those that didn't cooperate have not," concluded Henry Tillson. "As I hear from all sides, the, uh, Indian tribes are acting up."

And it was this last that finally brought a laugh to the group. To everyone's relief.

It only took a few minutes for the gathering to say good-bye to each other. They had already done the social thing the evening before, with drinks, cigars, a fine dinner at the Laramie Club, and the ladies. Or, as Sir Cecil Broadhurst put it, playing his British to the hilt, "The Ladies, God bless 'em!"

Cecil was more than pleased. The meetings had gone extremely well over the past couple of days, and he had firmed up his position with the others. He had also firmed up his own plan for the future, as he told himself while waiting for the stage to take off that afternoon.

Now, as the driver whipped his team out onto the trail heading north and west toward Stoneville, he let his thoughts play on the future. The whole deal was going to cost the Liverpool boys plenty. They would get what they wanted, he could assure them of that. It was all open and aboveboard. It was all on the table. They would get all that they were asking for. And they would necessarily pay for it. They would pay plenty.

Cecil smiled.

And he would get what he wanted.

The old prospector was clearly ancient—beyond counting, if anyone had asked him. Not that he wasn't spry. He was short, thin, leathery, tanned, burned, marinated by the sun, scrubbed by the wind, the search. Slocum knew the type. They had formerly dotted the West, though it did seem these days there were fewer, for the precious metal they sought had been found—and spent. There just couldn't be that much left, Slocum reasoned. And so it had to be that their numbers had decreased. As with the mountain men. As with the trappers. And pretty soon he knew it would be the same for the cowboys. The only good thing that seemed to be on the increase was the whores. Otherwise, there was a vast increase in businessmen, Bible drummers, politicians, newspapermen, slick operators, and con men. As Ulysses Gulbenkian had put it to him just recently, "The great ship of the Old West is vanishing over yonder horizon—and it will be soon gone, and forever. Now the rats are taking over. The scum. You will see. The landgrabbers, the railroaders, the agents, the swindlers and promoters. The West is soon to become a slicker's game. Fact, it's about that already, my friend."

Slocum remembered these caustic words as he regarded the little old prospector, who couldn't have been much more than 110 pounds soaking wet. His clothes were patched, and they were much too big for him. Slocum figured he could have packed along another person inside his shirt and pants if he'd a mind to. But the old boy from time to time opened his mouth, which was all but hidden by hair, in a big grin, revealing brown stubs. And there was a definite glint in his eye as he stood with the small crowd in Main Street listening to the patent-medicine hawker.

"Take advantage, gents, and ladies too," intoned the sleek gentleman under the black derby hat that was too big for him and had to be supported by both his bent ears so that it didn't fall down over his eyes.

"Take advantage of Professor Oldfinger's Absolute Elixir! This medical miracle is known not only throughout the American West, but in the great cities of the East, not to mention Europe. I avow that this bottle that I am holding here in my honest hand is the greatest medical miracle of the age. Taken internally it will cure the cholera, boils, ringworm, swelled joints, indigestion. It will dismiss—I said dismiss!— consumption, wasting of the flesh, the croup, night sweats. Rubbed on the body—the human body— externally, it will bring youth to tired muscles and ligaments. Good for children, good for horses. It is the miracle of the age. And only twenty-five cents! Ladies and gents, two bits will bring you new health, as long as the bottle lasts. Now don't rush, don't crowd in!"

"I'll take a bottle of that there," the old prospector said, and he tossed a coin to the medicine man, who caught it neatly.

Some others now began to eye the rows of bottles of Professor Oldfinger's Absolute Elixir. Slocum was watching the little prospector, who was reading the label on the bottle, or—he wondered—maybe he was just pretending to. After a moment he uncorked the bottle, sniffed its contents, and raised it to the hole in his gray beard where presumably his mouth was. With the bottle just at his lips, the little old man paused. Then he lowered the bottle and nudged the burro at his side, who was covered with dust. "Reckon you could try a shot of this, Hiram." And without further ado he reached up and opened the burro's mouth by poking his thumb into the side of its jaw and poured in a sizable wallop of Oldfinger's Absolute.

The crowd had caught on to this maneuver now and had turned to watch. Hiram apparently swallowed the dark brown fluid, then opened his wide mouth and stretched out his long tongue and brayed loudly.

"Good enough," said the old man and, lifting the bottle in a sort of toast, he placed the opening in his own mouth and tilted his head back. The crowd watched, fascinated, as the man in the baggy pants drank nearly half the bottle before lowering it with a mighty gasp.

"By Jehosophat! By Jumping . . ." But he fell into a fit of wheezing and doubled almost to the ground, while the crowd stared in fascination. Then suddenly he straightened, sighing deeply, still holding the bottle and now looking at it as though it was a holy relic.

"Folks!" He looked around at the crowd, a magnificent smile on his old face. "Lemme just say one thing. And it is this! Elihu Hoskins is cured! By the ring-ding Harry, he is cured! Me, Elihu. Let me tell you I bin one hundred now for one whole month, but I am telling you I am feeling like I was only ninety! By George, you better get that stuff 'fore I buy it all up myself!" And he began digging into his trouser pockets.

Slocum found himself grinning as he watched the crowd shelling out for the Professor's Elixir. In only a few more moments, the medicine hawker had cleaned a tidy sum and now climbed up onto the front seat of his wagon, which was drawn by two mules, and was already snapping his reins. "We shall see each other in Paradise," he called out.

The words came distinctly to Slocum, who was watching the whole play carefully. He saw the look the medicine man gave the old prospector, and then to his surprise, as the wagon turned slightly to get out into the center of Main Street, he caught the profile of a woman seated beside the medicine hawker. A turned-up nose, a smooth, concave cheek, and the curve of a well-molded bosom.

"See you be one of them fellers don't need elixir," said the shrewd voice at his elbow. The words were followed by a gravelly chortle as the old man sidled closer, scratching into his beard.

"Seems it keeps you healthy and young, mister," Slocum said with a grin.

"You be John Slocum, the new marshal of this town what claims he ain't."

"And you?"

"Elihu Hoskins, prospector still going on his big strike."

"And shill for yonder medicine man, I do believe." Slocum chuckled to show his words were friendly. "You did a right good job, sir."

"Years of practice, son." He threw his head in the direction of his burro. "See, I can go the other way, too. Me and Hiram that is. I bin known to give some of that patent medicine stuff to Hiram an' when I does it a certain way, old Hiram, he'll up and fall down and stick his legs up in the air and bray like a jackass 'bout to cash in."

"I've heard of you, Elihu. I remember hearing

about you and Hiram, lets see . . . over in Medicine Fork."

The old man's eyes were sparkling as he chuckled, recalling the scene. "I get around, Slocum. I hear you bin axin' about a feller named Bill sending for some friend of his and family and they got wiped out by the Injuns. That be correct?"

Slocum nodded.

"Bill got another name?"

"No. And I'm not even sure it's Bill. It could be Will."

The old man stared into the near distance and pursed his lips. "You got this from the kid?"

"It was in a letter he had in his pocket. Except the letter was all smudged with blood, and not that easy to read."

They had started to move down the street, but after another stretch of silence the old man said he needed a drink.

"That elixir doesn't last long, huh?" said Slocum.

"Thing is it gives a man's gut a good base for the real thing," Elihu said. "You care to join me, Slocum, I will ask you to pay for the both of us."

"I had already figured that, mister. I wasn't born yesterday," Slocum added with a laugh.

"Nor today, it 'pears," said the old-timer sardonically as they entered Harry Skull's place.

Slocum hadn't fooled himself into thinking he was going to get much out of Elihu Hoskins, and he was right. But he did try. He learned that the old boy was still hoping to make a strike, and that now and again he supplemented his living expenses—which were meager to be sure—with chores such as swamping out one of Stoneville's saloons, or in the present scene, shilling for the snake-oil salesman.

"Know who that woman was?" Slocum asked casually.

"Which?"

"The one with the medicine hawker."

"That one you was ogling?"

Slocum grinned. "Hell, I never even saw what she looked like. She was here and gone."

"You saw enough to feel it, son. And myself sure enough too." And the old boy clicked his tongue a few times, dropped a wink, and reached for his glass. "Hell, son, you be too young to appreciate the real good stuff. Takes a man of experience."

"Like yourself."

The old prospector lowered one eyelid like a window shade and clicked his tongue in appreciation of Slocum's sage observation.

"You're sure there isn't anything around the country that a man might find worth looking into, then," Slocum said after a while when they'd been talking about the closing of the mines.

"Nary a thing I know of."

"Then why are you prospecting?" Slocum came back at him like a whip.

The old man started to cackle. "Knowed you wuz gonna come at me with that. I just knowed it!"

"Well, why are you wasting your time prospecting here? Why don't you go to California, Montana? I mean, you say there isn't any gold around here, that it's all run out and the mines are dead. So what are you doing here, then?"

They were on the third round now, and while Slocum had been watching himself, he could tell that Elihu was feeling the whiskey.

"Why am I still here is what you're askin'?"

"That's what I'm asking."

"That's simple. Any fool could see why."

"Why?"

"On account of looking around here it's near home. While if I go to Californy, it's a damn far piece from home. That's why. Fer Chrissake, any damn fool could've figgered that!" And he reached furiously for his drink.

While Slocum's jaw fell open in amazement.

It was late when they parted company, and Slocum had come to the realization that Elihu Hoskins was neither as dumb nor as drunk as he looked. Elihu Hoskins was a smart bird, who had a damn good notion of what he was doing. And whatever that was, Slocum had a good notion the old man was onto something.

Only what? It occurred to him that he might be working for the law. He'd heard of stranger things than a hundred-year-old man playing prospector for the law. But why, and how, and for whom? All these questions were buzzing in him as he walked down to the livery and fed his horse.

On his way back to the Jersey Hotel he suddenly decided to stop in and see how Fidget was doing, while at the same time having a few moments with Annie Hardy.

He had just decided what he was going to do when he heard the wagon coming down the street and then saw it in the late-afternoon light. The interesting thing, and Slocum had noted this when he was watching the medicine man in action, was that the team of horses was first class. They were not at all the kind of moth-eaten crowbaits one usually saw pulling a carnival or medicine show wagon. They were a spanking pair of steel-gray geldings. And Slocum knew full well that whoever was pitching that elixir sale had to be making money somewhere else at the same time.

Without even thinking, he turned and started back to the livery. And as the wagon with those paired, high-stepping horses came by him he saw the man who was handling the team, and seated beside him the blonde, the one he'd seen previously right after Elihu's pitch had started the sales rolling.

When he walked into the livery, he made a pretense of tending to his spotted horse while the man and woman spoke to the hostler, who had suddenly appeared.

"I'll be back in the morning," the man was saying, and Slocum saw him handing the hostler money. "You take good care of the team and I'll see that you won't regret it."

Was there a threat in those words? Slocum wondered. The man, he noted, had an English accent. And so did the woman, whose name, he learned, was Cynthia.

When they walked by where he was pretending to give the spotted pony a rubdown he heard the man say, "Cecil will be amused to hear how it went."

And they were gone.

Slocum waited a small length of time and then

started back up the street toward Annie Hardy's house.

He had already decided that he was going to follow Elihu Hoskins, who he saw had taken his burro Hiram and left town. But he was going to wait a while so that the old man would be pretty sure that his backtrail was clear.

"Your dad lives by himself?" Slocum asked.

"He does. He likes it that way, I think. Although there are times when he spends the night. Comes for supper, feels tired, or falls asleep in the rocker there, and so he spends the night."

They were sitting in the front room, and she had cooked him supper, which they both had enjoyed along with Fidget. Then the boy had gone outside while Slocum helped wash the dishes.

"He hasn't said anything yet, I reckon," Slocum said when they sat down.

"Not a word. But I know very well he hears and knows what's going on."

"You've done well with him, I can see that."

"And he has done well for me," she said, and looked down at her hands lying in her lap.

He thought she looked marvelous. Her sadness brought a softness that seemed to blend into the room as the sunlight outside faded rapidly toward night.

"Is there anything I can do?" he said. "Do you need any money? I mean—for him?"

"Thank you. We're doing all right." She shifted her weight in her chair. "I'll be taking on some work soon. Some sewing. That will bring in money. No, we're doing just fine, thank you."

"Well," he said, "as you likely have guessed, I haven't any news on his family. Gulbenkian, the newspaperman, has sent out messages to Fort Fitz-william, Cheyenne, Laramie, and a few other places over the telegraph. But nothing has come of it. I've been asking everybody around."

"I know. I know, you've been doing all you can. And, understand, I am very happy to have Fidget here. Believe me. So I am in no hurry for him to go."

"Good, then. He's in good hands." And he smiled at her.

For a moment she held his eyes, and then she dropped hers.

"Please come by again," she said as she walked him to the door.

"I surely will."

Then, suddenly he leaned forward and kissed her. It was a quick, light kiss on the lips. And he felt his heart jump.

There was just an instant when they were to-gether, when she accepted his kiss, and he would have given a lot to stay there. But she backed away from him.

She stood in front of him still, and he didn't feel her hardening toward him. There was just a sorrow in her that was quite tangible.

"I—I'm sorry," she said.

"What for? You wanted to, and so did I."

"It's—soon."

"I'm in no hurry," Slocum said.

They looked directly at each other now, and there were tears standing in her eyes.

"Thank you," she said. "Thank you, John Slocum . . . for being my friend."

At the Broadhurst home the laughter rang off the oiled log walls and across the well-stocked supper table, as wines were served, and then, along with coffee and cigars, a fine Sazerac brandy.

Cynthia was in her element. She was a born hostess, an excellent cook who had the double ability of teaching a servant the appropriate ways of preparing meals, and could coax even the laziest menial to take good care of a house, cook meals, and attend to the endless minutiae of the home, such as cleaning, preparing, clearing away, and mostly remaining more or less invisible and keeping one's mouth closed about what went on in the higher echelons of the Western world. No one appreciated her more than Sir Cecil— Seal—who felt her support in so many ways, especially during some of the more arduous undertakings in his colorful career.

As now. There was a delicacy to the situation that the people in his employ had no possible way of understanding, yet Cynthia understood immediately. Only a hint was necessary, and sometimes not even that. She, like Cecil, was born to excitement.

Their guest and business associate also appreciated Cynthia's talents in the domestic field. Archibald Holmes, unlike Cecil, had been born to the higher social echelons. Cecil had been as it were "educated" into them. What he knew he had learned, and he had never really rid himself wholly of a slight lower-class accent. But Archie had not been educated to the higher level of society, he'd been born to it.

The three of them had always made a good team.

"I almost died laughing when that old prospector got going," Cynthia was saying again, as she embellished on the story of Elihu Hoskins and his burro.

"You recall the time when you fed the elixir to that woman's dog in Cheyenne, don't you, Archie?" Cecil said, hardly able to contain his laughter as he reviewed the scene of the dog taking a sip of elixir and keeling over with a growl.

"I recall how it wasn't so damn funny getting out of town," Archie said.

"All the same," Cynthia cut in, dabbing at her eyes with her tiny handkerchief, "*c'était le sport*, or however the French put it."

"Indeed," said Cecil. "It was good sport. What the hell, isn't that what we're all in it for? Not the money, the sport!"

And suddenly he jumped out of his chair, fell on his knees, with his hands clasped in prayer and his eyes raised toward heaven: "I didn't mean that, Lord! I didn't mean it!"

His two companions roared with laughter at the scene, Archie all but falling out of his chair.

Gasping, they reached for their drinks, wiping their eyes and finally sighing at what a good time they were having.

"Are we . . . are we sure Tanya is gone?" Cecil asked after a moment. "We don't want our cook to see what utter fools we are."

"She's gone," Cynthia said.

Then, as if by signal, all three fell silent.

"Good," said Cecil finally. "Now we must apply our brains to the big event that is coming up."

"Quite." Archie Holmes nodded. "Quite."

Cynthia reached for the Sazarac and poured. "We saw the man Slocum, Seal."

"And . . . ?"

She grinned wickedly at him. "He's exceedingly handsome."

"Well, so am I," said Archie. "What has that to do with anything? I mean, we are talking business now." And his tone was not joking.

"Sorry." She bit her lower lip, reprimanded and knowing she had earned it.

"I've sent out a geologist and a surveyor. You know, the usual sorts of experts," Cecil said.

"Yes, you wrote that you were planning that." Archie nodded.

"The area they investigated was that block where the company is planning to buy."

"You've been encouraging them to buy that section," Archie said.

"Right. It will unite all the sections we've picked up so that we'll have one solid spread for a whole helluva lot of cattle to feed and fatten before shipment."

"And—the other?" Archie said softly, taking out a cigar and sniffing it.

"I have, I believe, succeeded in discouraging Liverpool from purchasing that."

"You're talking about the section along Willow Creek," said Cynthia. "Is that right, Seal?"

Cecil nodded. "I told them it's largely rock, and moreover pointed out that it would be good politics to leave it. Not to buy up everything. Not to be greedy. We will show ourselves as only wanting something that we really need. We're not here to gobble up the whole country for Liverpool. Etcetera, etcetera."

"I'm sure you did it well, my boy!" Archie was grinning. "And now what?"

"Let me have one of your cigars," Cecil said.

Without a word, Archie reached into his coat pocket and brought out another cigar and handed it to his host.

"Cynthia, I hope you don't mind?" Cecil said.

"I was just going to suggest that I join you. You do know how much I love a good smoke."

When they had all lighted up, Archie released a satisfied sigh. His eyes flicked teasingly to Cynthia. "Back to Slocum," he said. And then abruptly, like a falling shutter, his whole attitude changed. Suddenly he was steel and stone.

The woman felt a shudder go through her, and she looked over at Cecil, who had also hardened. But she was used to Seal. Seal didn't frighten her as once in a while Archie did. Like now.

"Yes. Slocum." Cecil studied the ash forming on the head of his cigar.

"You may have found the man attractive, my dear," Archie said. "But *I*—I found him dangerous. And I want to suggest to you right now, and for your own good, that you start immediately to see him in that light."

"I have heard," Cecil said quietly, "that he might be—and very possibly is—working for either one of the big mining companies, or the government."

"I've heard he's roughed up a number of rough boys in town," Archie said.

"He has indeed. He's a cool customer."

"And dangerous," repeated Archie. "I've heard too that he might be working with that newspaperman, as a sort of reporter. But of course that would be simply a cover."

By now Cynthia had been dropped from the conversation, as it took on its new tone. She continued to sit there, however, as she had often enough before in other situations of this kind, smoking her cigar and listening. Later she would tell Cecil whatever she might have heard of a special nature—in intonation, pause, facial expression, or gesture of hands or body. Cecil found her invaluable in this respect.

"What do you suggest?" Archie said after a little while.

"Dicer is here," Cecil said.

"I see." Archie looked carefully at his companions. "Where is he, actually?"

"At Red Rock."

"But can you trust him?"

"No," Cecil said.

The ash from his cigar had spilled onto his coat, but he hadn't noticed. After a moment Cynthia leaned over and with her handkerchief brushed it off.

It didn't take long for Slocum to catch up with the old prospector. He had made camp just off the trail leading toward Owl Creek and Feather Butte. Slocum kept his distance, and in only a short while he saw that Elihu was breaking camp.

There was nothing secretive about Elihu, or so it seemed to Slocum. There often was that aspect of secretiveness around other prospectors. They were obviously afraid that someone would discover where they'd made a strike, or where they were going to make one.

Elihu did a lot of talking to himself, as Slocum discovered when he got closer to the camp in the pre-dawn as the old man was packing his burro. Of course, many old sourdoughs talked to themselves.

What had stuck in Slocum's mind was something that he had first heard from Gulbenkian, but also as part of the general saloon talk in town—that the mines were done for. That every vein had petered out. The glory days of the bonanzas were ended. Now it was strictly leavings. So what was Elihu Hoskins up to?

Cattle was the business now, and sheep. Sure there was always the trouble over the grazing, but the money was in livestock. Yes, the Black Hills had gold, and for sure California, but this wasn't anywhere near either place. This was a country that had been mined out. So what then was the old prospector doing? Dreaming of a strike? At least he had sense enough to pick up some money shilling.

Along about noon Slocum saw that the man he was following had stopped. The old prospector apparently suspected nothing, for he hadn't checked his backtrail at all. At the same time, it had become clear to Slocum that the man had a definite destination in mind. He wasn't just wandering around with his burro looking for sign of the precious metal, he was aiming for some special place, and shortly Slocum realized what it was. Elihu was heading toward Handy Mountain. And John Slocum wondered momentarily if he had any connection with the bandit gang at Red Rock. Yet there appeared no clear reason why he should.

But there was no time for speculating, for the old man, having unpacked some grub and eaten it, was now on his way again. It was late afternoon. And now to Slocum's surprise Elihu and Hiram broke away from the trail to Handy Mountain, which could be seen in the distance, and headed due west.

As they moved farther west Slocum's suspicions began to grow. Who was this old man? He was in one sense obviously an old prospector. On the other hand, he was obviously not looking for gold. He was heading somewhere, and he appeared to know where he was going. At the same time, he seemed quite unaware that someone was trailing him.

The trail had thickened through scrub oak, and Slocum was forced to move slowly so that his approach wouldn't carry sound ahead to the old man. But, judging by the contour of the land, he figured they could be coming close to something. The trail was not well used, and as it got narrower and more difficult for Slocum to ride, he had to dismount and lead his horse.

Every now and again he stopped and listened. Sometimes he could hear the old man and the burro up ahead.

The trail began to widen, and the timber had thinned. He could see sky ahead, and not only straight overhead as formerly. He felt they must be reaching their destination.

On an impulse Slocum decided to change his direction, and swiftly checking his own backtrail, he led his horse off the trail and into deep timber. He waited, but nothing appeared. He was about to return to the trail when something told him to wait.

In a moment a horse and rider came down the trail.

They were moving quickly—evidently the man felt no suspicion that anyone else would be there. He was riding in the same direction the old prospector was heading. And for an instant Slocum thought it was an Indian. The man was naked to the waist, and dark. He was wearing Indian leggings and moccasins, but he was not Indian. He could have been a half-breed. He was riding a saddled horse, not an Indian pony.

Slocum waited another few moments until he felt the trail was clear, and then slowly, on foot, leaving his pony tied to a tree, he slipped soundlessly through the timber and back to the trail. He stopped, listened, without a single muscle in his body moving, without a single thought in his mind other than what he was right now doing. Then he continued very slowly along the trail in the direction that Elihu Hoskins had been unwittingly leading him.

He heard Hiram, the burro, before he saw him. The animal was moving about in the brush and timber at the side of the trail where it began to open out.

And then he saw Elihu. The old man was lying just off the trail. He was lying face-down, but had evidently been able to crawl a few feet after being struck by the arrow that was sticking out of his back.

Slocum came up to him. "Take it slow," he said firmly. "Lie still, try to stay soft."

"Jesus," gasped the man on the ground. "Where the hell you been?"

"I'm going to try to pull it out."

"Goddamnit, never mind trying. Do it!"

"You got any booze on you?"

"In the pannier on Hiram—the elixir. Hurry it!"

Slocum let the old man have a stiff drink, then he swiftly cut open his shirt and sloshed some elixir around the wooden shaft where it protruded from the prospector's back. Then he placed his own rolled bandanna in Elihu's mouth and with all his strength pulled on the arrow. The old man didn't let out a sound, though Slocum could all but hear his body screaming. But he got the arrow out. He poured some elixir into the wound and then bound it.

Elihu Hoskins had passed out.

Slocum studied the arrow. The butt end was whittled to a sharp ridge, with the string notch perfectly centered. The butt tapered to the shaft, and the triangular head had absolutely straight sides. The shaft was slender, and there were no barbs on the arrows. He looked at the three wavy lines running from the head of the shaft to the feathers. He knew these were the spirit lines communicating with the Great Mysterious, and he remembered the old Indian telling him how the good medicine flowed along wavy lines. He knew it was a Cheyenne arrow. And the Cheyenne were nowhere near here.

But by God, he was thinking. By God, when he'd pulled out the arrow that one-hundred-year-old man hadn't let out a sound!

* * *

"We're lucky it didn't go in all that deep," Slocum said after he had laid Elihu down on the bed in Annie Hardy's spare room. "That feller who shot you—if he'd been Indian you wouldn't be with us."

The old man tried a smile, but he was still in pain even though Doc Entwhistle had administered pain-killer.

"He's got to lie still. I mean still," Doc said to Annie and Slocum.

"I'll see to it." She pulled a sheet up over Elihu, who was lying on his stomach, and tucked it around his shoulders.

Elihu's eyes were closed. He was out of it again. Before passing out he'd been out of his head, bab-bling about Indians, gold, bandits, a big strike, and a lot of mumbo-jumbo talk that nobody could under-stand. In fact, only those words that were intelligible caught their attention, but there were no sentences that linked them with any meaning.

"He's off his head," Doc said. "What do you ex-pect? An old sourdough like that, prospecting his whole life, and it's all he thinks about—striking it high, wide, and handsome."

They had moved out to the parlor, and Annie of-fered coffee.

"Thank you, yes," Entwhistle said. "Principally because of the excuse to enjoy your delightful com-pany, my dear."

Annie went to him and put her hand on his arm. Slocum could see that there were almost tears in her eyes. He had heard from Kneecaps how Entwhistle had helped her through her husband Clay's murder.

And at that very moment he felt something of himself going out to her.

She turned and looked at him. "Would you like some coffee?"

"I sure would."

Later, after having had supper with Annie and her father, he walked back to the Jersey Hotel and discovered that somebody had broken into his room and searched his war bag. Nothing was missing. He cross-examined the room clerk, a not very bright young man, and found out nothing. And so, without asking permission or even notifying the man at the desk, he found another room in the house and locked himself in. That night he slept as he would have on the trail, only deep enough to get some rest, but lightly enough so that the slightest disturbance would wake him.

When he awakened in the morning he remembered that after bringing in Elihu he had gone to his hotel and changed his pants, which had blood on them, before returning to the Hardy house for supper. The letter with the blood smears had been in one of the pockets. And now it was gone.

As he walked down to the cafe where he had planned to have breakfast he decided that he was glad it had happened. And when he ran into Ulysses Gulbenkian at the cafe he told him so.

"Why, for Christ sakes?" the newspaperman asked, spluttering into his coffee.

"Because now I know for sure that there's something going on a lot deeper than meets the eye."

"How do you mean?"

"I mean I do believe somebody knew that the boy

and his family, whoever they were, were coming out here, and there was something in that letter saying why. Whoever ordered that wagon train massacre was not only trying to stop the person or persons getting here, but also didn't want something known."

"What about the stampede you told me about? And the trouble on the Texas trail coming north that everybody's been having?"

"Same thing. Somebody doesn't want those herds here. And somebody didn't want Fidget's bunch here either. For some reason or other, someone's been hell-bent on keeping people away from Stoneville and this part of the country."

Ulysses looked sour at that, as he stabbed at a piece of steak and rubbed it around in his egg.

For several moments they were silent with their thoughts and their food.

Finally Gulbenkian leaned forward on the table and looked Slocum right in the eye. "Well," he said. "They sure fucked up, whoever it was, or is. On account of they might have got rid of those others but they ended up with Slocum." He shook his head in mock sorrow. "The goddamn fools!"

"Maybe it's Fidget they can thank for that," Slocum said.

"Fidget!"

"You know, the more I look at that kid the more I see he's got the makings of a real good trailsman."

"You goddamned asshole! Do you see what you done!" Cecil's fury broke straight across the room into the huge body, neck, face, and especially the nose of Big Nose Hendry. So exercised was Sir Cecil

Broadhurst that he had totally lost his role of English lord, to the extent of returning wholly to his native accent, which he found infinitely more satisfactory for delivering invective to a lesser person.

"You can't even carry out a simple order, you stupid piece of shit! You were told to have the old man followed! Do you hear that? Followed!"

"I told Cola that. I tolt him!"

"Then how come he fucked up, the idiot!"

"Cola don't understand English so good. I dunno. I tolt him to follow."

"You've been told, everyone has been told that the Indian business is finished. That was just to throw confusion, so's nobody'd be sure who was doing what. And, for Christ sake, you've now drawn everybody's attention to that part of the country. Goddamn it, goddamn it, goddamn it!" Cecil's right fist pounded into the palm of his left hand as he bore down on those words.

"Shit," muttered Big Nose, his big head hanging, his huge eyes searching the corners of the room for help. "Well, least he ain't dead," he said finally.

"Are you sure?" said the short, muscular-looking man in the tight-fitting white silk shirt, black broadcloth coat, and California pants who was seated across the room, almost against the wall.

Big Nose looked up. "Slocum, I heard, brung him in, got him to Entwhistle, and now he's at McFadden's daughter's place."

"Our former marshal's widow." Cecil's sour words dripped into the scene as he glared at Big Nose.

"Big Nose, don't never again do anything—*any-*

thing—without you first speak to me or Mr. Broad-hurst. You understand me?"

The voice of the man in the chair was soft, but it held the quality of menace that a man like Big Nose Hendry could understand.

Big Nose nodded. Sir Cecil smiled a tight, appreciative smile. It was of course why he had Dicer on the payroll. The reason for having Big Nose on the payroll was sometimes—as now—a question. Yet the man was excellent with the Red Rock men. He was totally loyal, and save for the two encounters with Slocum, he was absolutely invincible. The fact that he was stupid was a drawback. Yet at the same time Cecil was fully aware of the dangers in having a man about who was too intelligent. For instance, a man like Dicer.

Dicer never raised his voice. He never got excited. The man saved his force for the moments that were, as he put it himself, more "ultimate." Dicer liked that phrase. He had learned it at an early age from his father, shortly before that famous killer's death by hanging. It was one of the good things Dicer senior had left his son. The other legacy was a gun arm as swift as thought. It was an arm whose speed and accuracy were unalloyed by even the slightest sense of right and wrong. An arm that was wholly expedient.

Cecil was realizing these things too as he watched Dicer. For, in a way, the man fascinated him. He had known and dealt with killers in his time, even famous ones. Yet none like Dicer. Well, it was the deal: Big Nose for muscle, and handling the men, and Dicer for the extermination of whatever was in

the way. And of course himself as mastermind behind everything. Assisted by Archie and Cynthia.
Cecil was a philosopher, meaning he was practical in
the face of adversity. For instance, now he was able
to face this stupid mistake, for a mistake could
always be turned into a lesson.

"Whoever is ultimately to blame," Cecil said,
more calmly now, and definitely more "English,"
"yourself or Cola, will definitely not make such an
error again. You will make that absolutely clear to
Cola. Neither you nor this man will make another
mistake. This mistake with the old man was your
last."

"It can be handled," Dicer said, speaking softly
through his thin lips. He had removed his hat, and
his slick black hair shone like patent leather in the
afternoon sunlight coming through the window.

"I know that. I know that," Cecil said impatiently.
"Hell, man, anything can be 'handled.' The question
is the manner in which it is handled. Not this damn
bungling!" He shook his head as though to get rid of
what he was thinking. "However, the damage is
done. Let's get on with it." He stood before the two
of them, ticking off the points on his fingers.
"Number one, I want to know the exact progress of
the old prospector. Number two, I want to know the
movements of John Slocum. Number three, I want
the Hardy woman watched, and her father. And
Number four, I want a sharp eye kept on that newspaper fellow."

"Gulbenkian," Big Nose said helpfully.

"I happen to know his name, thank you, Mr. Google."

A silence fell, and finally Cecil said, "That will be all for now."

Big Nose turned to the door, opened it, and went out.

"I'd like a word," Dicer said. He was standing now, and since he was wearing a rather loose coat, no weapons were visible; that is, he wore a gun in a shoulder holster, another inside his shirt, a belly gun, but nothing at his hips. To the average person looking at him he appeared unarmed. A number of people had not lived to repeat that error.

"Shut the door then," Cecil said, and he walked around his desk and sat down.

Dicer shut the door and remained standing. "Slocum," he said.

"Yes." Cecil leaned forward on his desk, his eyes looking right at the man he had hired at a handsome fee, and thus far had had no regrets about. "Yes," he repeated. "Slocum, as you see, will have to go."

"It won't be a problem."

"Only insofar as it must look all right to the general public and the law in Laramie and Fort Fitzwilliam."

"I will carry that in mind."

"But not yet," Cecil said. "As you know, while there is no marshal or sheriff in Stoneville, people are beginning to think of Slocum in that regard. Now then, with a half-dozen men of the law dispensed with already, we have to go slowly. Whatever happens, that is to say, must be open and aboveboard.

An accident, a gun duel, even a beating or two. I wouldn't object to a pistol-whipping." He paused, watching the clouded eyes of the other man. "You understand me. No drygulching, no ambush. That last one with that Hardy fellow, it went down hard with a lot of people. And at this point in our, uh, negotiations, we don't want any adverse feelings. There must not be the shadow of suspicion directed toward myself—or the company."

His eyes moved across the impassive face of the man standing before him. "I want you to keep in close touch with me about this, Dicer. You understand?"

"There's a quick way to settle Slocum," Dicer said, his mouth hardly moving as he spoke.

"Yes, but there is one thing for you to remember. And it is this: I make the decisions here. And another point to keep in mind is that while you obviously would like to put down a man of Slocum's stature and reputation, don't forget that in Boot Hill they don't accept American money—of which you will have rather a great deal only when our arrangement is concluded." Cecil looked down at his hands, reached for a paper on his desk, and without looking up said, "That should be enough for the present."

When he heard the door close he looked up, his face wreathed in a happy smile. Quickly he rose and walked across the room to a second door and opened it.

"My dear Cynthia! Fancy meeting you here!"

"I heard it all," she said happily. "Darling, you were marvelous. Absolutely marvelous."

"I have some other marvels to show you, my darling." And he slid his arms around her. "I am in the mood for celebrating."

"That's two of us."

"Three," Cecil said, as he took out his rigid member and placed it in her hand.

7

"What I'm looking for is a map, if there is such a thing," Slocum said as he walked into the office of the Stoneville *Quarrier*.

The owner, publisher, editor, and principal reporter and feature writer of Stoneville's lone news sheet looked up from the chaos of papers under which the open area of his rolltop desk had all but disappeared. His open palm now offered the pile of papers to his visitor.

"Welcome to help yourself. If you can find anything useful in there lemme know." And he dropped his eyes down to the paper he was holding in his other hand.

Then, looking up again over the steel-rimmed spectacles that hung halfway down his nose, he said, "Why not try the land office. They got maps growing up through the floorboards."

"It's private," Slocum said.

"You mean you don't want them to know what you're up to. Well, hell, then why didn't you say so in the first place?"

"Expected you to figure that out for yourself," Slocum said dryly.

Plunging his arm into the mountain of papers, Gulbenkian, his face stern with decision, said, "What particular area? I don't have any maps like a surveyor, like them land office scoundrels. But I did have something here."

"Up near Handy Mountain is where I'm interested."

"Got'cha!" And Ulysses yanked out a folded paper, spilling more documents on the floor, but ignoring them in the intensity of the moment.

"Handy Mountain, eh? Red Rock you're talking about!"

"No. Though I could use a map on that, too, if there was such a thing. But something around that area. Not the exact place where Big Nose and some of the boys are supposed to spend their time."

Gulbenkian had opened the paper he had retrieved from the pile and was studying it. "Don't reckon this'll do you, but take a look."

Slocum spread the sheet of paper on the floor and squatted near Ulysses so that they could both see it.

"That's Handy Mountain there," he said. "And I guess, well, maybe over here . . ." He moved his finger to the west of the mountain, and then south. "That looks to be a trail there."

A moment or two passed while both of them studied the map.

"It ain't very detailed," Ulysses said. "But it does show you the main points. I don't know who drew it. But I got some of them one time when I was running a story on range rights, I think it was. And, yes, it was with the sheep and cattle." He leaned back, squinting his face toward the ceiling. Then, suddenly, like a clenched fist that was suddenly released, his face sprang open. "The mines. It was something to do with the mines. Damn!" He turned to the desk. "I got it somewhere. But shit no. They busted the press and wrecked the office. I remember, I was looking for that once before. Right after those sons-ofbitches broke in here. Not so long ago, it was, and I wanted to take inventory of the damage. Shit, they done such a thorough job it took me only five minutes to see what I had left."

He cocked his eye quickly at Slocum now. "Why? What are you up to? You know, Slocum, I can tell you'd make one helluva lawman."

"Save the compliments, my friend." Slocum was still studying the map. Finally, he stood up and crossed to a chair that was against the wall and sat down.

"Well?" said Gulbenkian. "You going to come across with the big secret?"

"No secret. I'm just mighty curious why that old prospector and his burro were interested in that part of the country."

"That's what I figgered," Gulbenkian said, with a sharp look on his face.

"As I figure it, it ain't anywhere near good grazing, and it ain't near any mining."

"It ain't too far from where the Liverpool ran their herd through that time I told you about—right through Tom Spofford's spread. I'm talking about Cal Bowker and his Lazy Diamond riders."

Slocum got up quickly and crossed to the map,

which was still lying on the floor. "Show me," he said.

"Well, it'd be off this map," said Gulbenkian. "About like here, I'd reckon it." And with his middle finger he tapped the bare floor near the edge of the paper.

"But who's around here?" Slocum said, pointing. "I mean where the old man was arrowed."

"What do you mean 'who'? That's just open land. There isn't anybody around there."

"Now. All right, there is nobody there now. This here, on this side of the mountain. There was timber, but when I packed old Elihu back to town we came down some real nice grazing on the other side of the river. I mean it was good, lush feed. Lots of game, and not a sign of cattle, sheep, horses, or men. I would bet it wasn't tribal land. There weren't any signs of Indians anywhere around."

"Excepting the arrow that shot the old man."

"That was a fake."

Gulbenkian scratched himself. "What you're asking, sir, is why with such prime land for the taking, why wasn't it taken. Why was there no cabin, no stock grazing, no sign of life? Human life, that is. Right?"

Slocum had been squatting again and now he stood up. "Look, suppose that wall there in front of you was a map. And let's think of it as being round, roughly a circle, and this is the center. Here." He pointed. "This is Stoneville. This is the Colly Mine. This is the Gillis ranch, this is another outfit; I don't know the names. But you get my point. They're all around here. The mines, the ranches, and of course the Lazy Diamond, and some others that are about to be taken over by Liverpool. Or at least what they've got their eye on."

"My friend, I am getting your drift real clear!" Ulysses' face was shining with excitement.

"What I want to know is—"

"—why that piece of land has no one on it," said Gulbenkian, overlapping him in his excitement.

"Who owns it?"

"By God, there is something here. Something we had not seen." He put his cigar back in his mouth and slapped his thigh so hard he winced and the cigar ash fell all over his waistcoat.

"The land office will have it, for sure," Slocum said.

Ulysses Gulbenkian nodded briskly.

"And the minute I ask about it, or anyone asks about it, they'll be wondering why."

"Can you talk to the old man? Is he up to it?"

"He's not in any way to talk," Slocum said. "And he likely wouldn't anyway."

"You think he's onto something, and that's why he was out there?"

"I know he wasn't heading for the Red Rock bunch. And why else he was there I dunno."

"Maybe he was leaving the country?"

"Maybe. Maybe I'm looking for something that ain't there, but I want to follow it."

Gulbenkian leaned back in his chair, his cigar clamped in his jaws, thumbs hooked in his waistcoat. "I told you you'd make a good lawman, and I was right. You're just what Stoneville needs."

"Thanks," said Slocum, his words sour as vinegar. "Now, I want you to help me."

"I already am, sir. I already am planning how I will approach the land office."

"And get thrown out, shot, or have your press wrecked again."

"You are suggesting strongly, then, that there is subterfuge afoot."

"I am not suggesting anything," Slocum said firmly. "I'm only asking the question, What's with that package of land? Who owns it? Anyone? That's all. I might want to buy it, or homestead it, or run my herd on it. Who knows? A man can ask."

"But if you—"

"If I did that, the minute I asked, then if there was actually something crooked going on we'd be up the creek. And if there isn't, so all right then. But I want to find out on the quiet."

"You want it unbeknownst to anybody that it is you asking."

"You got it," Slocum said. "And by golly," he added with a big grin, "this town needs you, Ulysses. They need a good newspaperman like yourself to run the paper here. How about taking a crack at that!"

At this point Gulbenkian dissolved in roaring, watery laughter, the tears sprouting from his eyes, his shoulders shaking, while he slapped his thigh again and again, though not hard this time.

Suddenly a cry broke from the boy, and Slocum saw the streak of red tracing along his hand where the

knife had slipped off the piece of wood he was whittling and cut him.

"Well, I'll be darned if you can't come out with
some kind of sound!" Slocum said as he took the
knife and piece of wood from him. "Here, let me
take a look at her."

Slowly, Fidget moved his hand forward.

Slocum studied the cut. It wasn't all that deep,
and he reasoned it was more surprise than pain that
had caused the boy to call out. "She'll be all right.
Just hold your hand up for a while, that'll help stop
her. What bleeding's been done, that's washed it out,
and so she's clean." He bent closer to the boy's hand.
"Yep. Now hold your arm up. Like this." He raised
his own arm to show what he meant. "See, blood, it
moves like a creek, downstream, see. So you hold
your arm up she'll stay upstream more. She won't
move out so easily."

Fidget did as he was told, not uttering a word.
They sat in silence for a while. Slocum wanted what
had happened to sink into him. After a while Slocum
stood up and nodded at the boy and started to walk
away. He'd only gone a few yards when he felt the
boy behind him.

When he stopped and turned around he saw Fidget
had also stopped. He was still holding his hand up,
and Slocum saw that the bleeding had stopped.

"Come on, then," Slocum said. "We'll go down to
the livery. I got to look at my pony's shoes, and
maybe you can help me."

By now the news was current in Stoneville and other
towns of the northern area that there was more trou-

ble on the trails coming up from Texas. Indians, Comancheros, cattle thieves were hitting the herds, although it was also noted that certain herds managed
to escape the trouble. This observation was drawn to
the attention of Sir Cecil, who immediately sent
word to the proper quarters that those favored herds
should be allowed to undergo a certain harassment,
but harassment that was controlled. No one was to be
hurt, in other words. The exercise was only to quell
the rumors and questions about why certain herds
came up the trail unmolested.

Meanwhile, Slocum had taken the stage to Fort
Fitzwilliam and discovered nothing. The fort had no
records of land transactions in that area. When he
returned to Stoneville, Gulbenkian suggested a
break-in at the land office.

"Only as a last recourse," Slocum had told him.
"If anything went wrong we'd be finished. I'm going
to try just one more thing."

"What's that? What're you going to do?"

"I'm just going out to take a closer look around. I
couldn't do that when I was bringing Elihu in, and I
could have missed something."

"I want to go with you."

"You're crazy."

"That's certain. But I want to go. Two heads, two
pairs of eyes. Two. Two is twice one. Or is it better
to say, 'Two *are* twice one'? I favor the latter. It
must therefore be correct. What will we need?"

He had risen briskly and was looking about the
office. Slocum realized the man was determined. He
knew he could have stopped him, but then thought,
Why not? Another point of view might help.

"You'll need a horse. A gun. And we will need food and water. Let's get going."

"How long do you figure we'll be gone?" Ulysses asked, looking around his office.

"Couple days, a night or two at the most. Or"— and Slocum looked at his companion quietly—"it could be forever."

"On that cheerful note let us go," said Ulysses with a heavy voice.

In a moment he had locked up and they were walking down Main Street toward the livery.

"Last time I rented a sharp little strawberry roan. Hope I could get him again."

"On the other hand," Slocum said, "we might only be there a few hours."

"Nothing like certainty," Ulysses commented dryly. "A man needs to know where he stands."

As they rode away from the town, the sun was halfway through the middle of the forenoon. Hot, pale against the light blue sky, the two men felt it through their shirts and trousers.

"We'll go easy with the horses," Slocum said as they turned into the northern trail that led in the direction of Handy Mountain. "I've a notion we'll want them fresh when we get there, not played out."

The following morning they reached the open section of land that Slocum had described to Ulysses, the ground he had traversed on his way back to Stoneville with the wounded Elihu Hoskins. But there was nothing more to be seen, other than the trail leading through the timber at one end, and that looked to have been recently traveled.

Slocum had dismounted to check sign, and now he stepped again into his saddle, and without a word the two men started along the trail.

In about an hour the trail opened again into another flat area, which was much higher up than the previous one. Here, quite unexpectedly, they came on a burned cabin and barn, a ruined corral. The place was totally hidden by high timber, invisible from below, but with a view of the long, sweeping land leading down to the winding Stone River. Nearby, however, ran a creek lined with willows and box elders.

It was obvious to Slocum that the fire had taken place a good while ago, for the grass had grown over some of the fallen logs.

"I believe this could be the old Hogan place," Gulbenkian said. "I'd about forgotten it. And it wasn't on the map you drew on my wall."

"I've a notion it was this the old boy was heading for," Slocum said. "I mean, he was in fact moving all about, even going in an opposite direction to here, but when I caught up with him, he'd again come back to north."

Slocum took out a quirly and slowly lighted it, squinting against the smoke, with his eyes on his companion. "Who is Hogan?"

"He ain't around."

"I can see that. Why is this place burned? Looks like it might have been fired. Do you know anything about it?" He didn't wait for Ulysses to answer his questions, but now started to move about, his eyes on the ground. "I read more than just a fire. There are bullet holes in those logs."

He squatted suddenly, studying the ground. "Hard to tell much after such a length of time."

Suddenly he reached down and picked up a shell casing. "Spencer." He stood up and began walking. "Lots of horses. And I am guessing, but if the men who attacked, and I am saying there was a fight, if they had Spencers, what did the other side have?"

He stopped walking and nodded toward part of a cowhide lying on the ground where the corral had been. "Looks to me like it had some extra branding worked on it. See that tree yonder?" And he strode toward a big cottonwood that had a rope hanging from one of its branches. "See, they had something hanging here. I mean, a beef, not a man." He spat reflectively. "And somebody skinned it. That's a bullethole in this piece of hide here. But looky here." He was squatting. "See, two horses, recent." He stood up and pointed.

As he walked about the ruin picking up pieces of hide, a horseshoe, some more empty cartridge shells, and a rusted bowie knife, he kept talking, half to Ulysses and half to himself, making the story go, changing it as it needed correcting with new evidence, but piecing it all together.

"This here is another Arapaho arrowhead. But it's just lying here, like somebody dropped it or planted it to make it look like the Indians."

"It was whites and Indians both, I heard," Ulysses told him. "I was down in Miller City, about a year ago at least. I don't know if anyone ever got the straight of it. But a man name of Hogan had the place. Him and his wife. Hil Hogan." Ulysses stood still in the middle of what had once been the corral and squinted as his thoughts went back. "An Indian wipeout, as far as anyone could tell. At least that was the story I got when I got back to Stoneville, and I never had any reason to think otherwise."

"Maybe," Slocum said. "Maybe it was Indians. But there wasn't any big Indian trouble around here at that time, was there?" He squinted. "Funny. Almost like someone's been wanting us to think it's a fake. Same with the rubout at Moon Basin."

"Nothing big. Nothing like organized. But there were little troubles here and there. Cattle raiding, mostly, and some horse stealing. Nothing big, as I say. Mostly people figured it was young braves feeling their oats. No big wipeout. Nothing like what you ran into."

"And this? People figured it was just a raid?"

Gulbenkian nodded. He was feeling the heat and wiped his forehead with his shirtsleeve. "Funny thing, I remember now. About Hogan."

"What about him?"

They had squatted now, with their forearms on their thighs, as men did when talking, squatted in the place where the corral had been, with the brims of their hats pulled low over their eyes against the brilliant light of the westering sun. Turning his head, John Slocum spat reflectively at nothing.

Gulbenkian canted his head a little, trying to catch his memory of something. "Well," he said. "Hil Hogan was a tough man, so I heard. Fast with a gun, hard, made things disagreeable for anyone crossed him."

"Lot of men like that in this country," Slocum said dryly.

"Hil—Hildebrand his name was—Hil it seems was even more so. Often on the prod. But he kept his nose pretty clean. Didn't get crazy drunk like some down to Stoneville. Though he didn't mind tying one on now and again. But he was a loner. He kept to himself. Had a couple of hundred head, I believe I heard. But he didn't bide the big stockmen. And what the hell; who does?"

"That's right. Who does!" Slocum nodded in agreement.

"See, there was a bunch used to throw in with the big cattlemen, like Cal Bowker and his Lazy Diamond, when it came time to roundup and branding and shipping."

"And Hogan bucked—that it?"

"Hogan bucked. Said Bowker was cheating him or something. I don't remember all the details, but something like that. Anyway, Hogan got squared off against Bowker and the Liverpool outfit that backed him."

"You're saying Bowker and the Liverpool bunch did this?" Slocum nodded at the burned cabin, the remains of the corral.

"I am not saying, on account of I do not know. But I wouldn't be surprised."

"How long ago?"

Gulbenkian squinted, sniffed through his hairy nostrils, and pursed his lips in reflection. "I'd put it a year. About a year ago. No, make it a year and half."

"Where is Hogan now?"

"Dunno. Left the country. His wife died, I heard. Some say he hit the owlhoot trail. There were some cattle shot up at the Lazy D, and a couple of

Bowker's hands were busted all to hell when they ran into Hogan in one of the saloons in town. Then—what I heard—Hogan swore by God he was going to get Bowker and the whole of the Liverpool crowd. Yup." He nodded in affirmation as his memory came more into focus. "Hogan went outlaw. At least, that's the story that was heard. By God, I nearly forgot! There's a dodger out on him. Yup. Got it somewhere in that damn desk of mine back at the office."

"What's he wanted for?" Slocum asked, looking directly at Ulysses.

"Cattle rustling, horse thieving, pulling a gun on one of the Lazy Diamond men—I think it was Bert Bindler, the ramrod. But that part I am not so sure of. But we can look up that dodger."

"Thing is, where is Hogan now?"

With his elbows still on his knees, Gulbenkian spread his arms apart and shrugged. "You tell me." And he shook his head from side to side. "I'll tell you one thing, though. The man is said to be a crack shot. And—yes, I'd forgotten this bit—the word is that he used to be an outlaw before he came to this country. Up in Montana somewhere."

After a silence, during which the newspaperman built himself a smoke with his makings, Slocum spoke with his eyes on a design he was drawing in the dirt floor of what had been the corral. "How would it strike you if you heard that maybe Hogan was still around?"

He lifted his head and watched his companion's thick white eyebrows pop up.

"What the hell makes you say that? That sounds real crazy, I mean."

"Where would you hide, hide so you could still know what was going on with your place, if it was you, Ulysses?"

"Jesus, Slocum! Have you got any evidence for that? Sure, anybody can make a crazy wild guess, but how can you back up such a statement? Why, anyway, would Hogan want to hang around here when there's a price on his head? I mean, that's crazy!"

"Look, this here is—was—his place. Right?"

"That's what everyone took it to be."

"Bowker or his Liverpool friends, or both and all of them wanted Hogan out. Meaning they wanted this piece of land. Why?"

"I'd say, same reason they wanted—and got, goddamn them—Tom Spofford's place." Gulbenkian was scowling as he spoke.

"What would you do if you were Hogan?"

"Fight the sonofabitch!"

"How?"

"But Tom Spofford wasn't an outlaw. He didn't have a price on his head. He didn't have the law after him."

"True. But he was in the same mess with the Liverpool bunch."

"I get your drift. Course, Hogan did have the law on his ass."

"Up it," Slocum corrected. "And it appears to me he was alone. A loner, like you say."

"That still doesn't prove he hasn't left the country."

"Doesn't prove he did, or he didn't," Slocum said. "It isn't a matter of proof. I'm saying he could easily have come back, after his place was fired and people were used to him being away. It's not proof. It's good figuring."

"Then why didn't whoever it was wanted this place just move in and take it?"

"There were some lawmen about from time to time, weren't there? I mean, they do have to watch it a little bit, those big boys."

Ulysses nodded. "Right." Then his eyebrows arched in a serious question as he regarded Slocum face to face beneath their battered Stetson brims. "Then how do you read those two riders that were here, you say recently?" And he nodded to the place where Slocum had seen the tracks of the two horses.

"Except they weren't two riders," Slocum said.

"What do you mean. You just said . . ."

"One rider. One packhorse. See." He pointed. "If you study those tracks leading there, you'll see one horse was ridden, the other was being led."

"Jesus . . ." murmured the venerable newspaper-man, his eyes and mouth round with awe. "I just don't know how the hell you can read that stuff so easy!"

"All you got to do is see what's right in front of you," Slocum said. "Like for instance . . ." And he paused, squinting at the sky.

A moment passed.

"Like for instance . . . what?" Ulysses Gulbenkian asked.

Slocum said, "Like for instance, maybe Hil being like Bill."

"I never thought of that!" Ulysses ran his forearm across his face, wiping sweat.

"I have been thinking about it ever since you said the name, my friend."

"You think maybe that letter was written by . . ."

"Drop your voice," Slocum said, with a tight look in his eyes.

Gulbenkian shifted his weight.

"Don't get up yet," Slocum said, hardly moving his lips, and with his eyes directly on the other man.

"What the hell . . . ? I'm stiffening up. Got a game leg, I . . ." But something in Slocum's look stopped him from whatever he was going to say.

"Don't move," Slocum said, his eyes on the ground, and speaking almost in a whisper. "Act natural. And don't make any fast moves and don't reach for anything."

"But . . ."

"Remember—you wanted to come along, my friend."

"What the hell are you talking about?" But he had lowered his voice.

"I'm talking about the man standing just inside that line of spruce yonder. He's got the sun at his back, and you and me, we've got it in our eyes, so I can't see what kind of a gun he's got. But ten will get you twenty that whatever it is, it's pointed right at us."

8

Sometimes the long view across the nearly empty plain had appeared to shimmer, and viewing was tricky. To anyone who might happen to have been watching, the horse and rider now appeared indistinguishable from the stand of pine and fir. It was only in movement, as they broke out of the horizon and rode down into the plain, that they became clear.

They had moved slowly, the rider watching for sign, noticing the jay sweeping into the sky as it broke from the willows down by the river. The man's body realized the bird's movement at the same instant as his eyes, and everything in him, sharpened.

Shifting in his heated saddle, he eased the .45 Schofield that was holstered at his right hip, touched the hideout derringer inside his shirt. Yet he did not change the slow gait of the bay gelding as it quartered down to the plain.

In a while they had found cover again in the willows at the edge of the river. The rider drew rein. When he saw the coyote he knew why the jay had broken cover. Still, he maintained his alert. Shifting a little in his stock saddle, he reached to the pocket of his sweat-stained shirt and took out a cheroot. He lighted it, after striking the wooden lucifer on the saddle horn. But he didn't throw away the match, he put it into his shirt pocket.

Close up he was a stocky, muscular man of average height, not old, not young, maybe in his forties, yet with the mark of experience in his dark face. Beneath his widely spaced gray eyes lay the marks of crow's-feet. He leaned forward onto the pommel of his saddle now, his arms crossed, peering out from the dense protection of the willows to study the land about him.

He let himself enjoy the cheroot, though he did not let go of his alertness. The cheroot was good. It had been a real long wait, and he knew he was getting restless. Knowing himself well, he knew that he had to be careful—especially careful at such a moment. Since he'd come back he had not dared to show himself in the town, and so he'd been living off the land. Good enough, except with nothing in the way to drink, and no women, no cards or dice. And besides that, he hadn't been able to hunt, for he only had the two handguns, and not a great deal of ammunition.

Well, he'd had to pull out of where he'd camped when the riders came. It had been close, for he'd been expecting the old man, but it had been the riders. Three of them. He'd figured them out by the sound. He'd always been good with sound. And besides he knew the country. He'd been over every inch of it, not only with the cows but checking everything back when he'd moved in, and the trails in and out, especially that climb over the top of the rimrocks, which had to be on foot, though you could lead a horse, a tough one, if you were lucky.

He hadn't expected the three riders. It had been a week ago. They were cowmen, and he recognized one: Bowker, riding a little dappled gray with that Lazy Diamond brand on its shoulder. He knew the brand, for sure. He'd changed it with his running iron more than a few times. And he saw the three were well armed. All were packing sidearms, and there was a saddle gun to boot with each horse. It was not the time for confrontation. Well, maybe they'd noticed something, he had decided. Maybe they'd spotted his latest branding, or re-branding of the Lazy Diamond beef. The sonsofbitches!

He should have waited. It had been a mistake, especially now. Especially with the old buzzard coming out to help him. Only he'd needed the beef. He had to eat. Especially with his own cows run off. No, on second thought it was good. It would shake them.

He grinned. Maybe it hadn't been such a mistake. Yes, that was it. They would be checking on their precious beef. Wasn't that the way he'd planned it? Pick the sonsofbitches to pieces. Worry 'em! Hell, he must be getting loose in the head, starting to worry. Like the old man. Well, no question about it, he missed the action. He missed the girls and the cards and dice, and the boys. Though, not so much the boys. Hell, he'd always been a loner and he sure wasn't going to switch his horse now. No, by God! For sure! For sure, not with everything so close. But, by God he did need somebody to help. The old man was too old, too crazy.

Well, he had fought them when they came and
fired the place. By God, there must've been twenty
of them. Maybe more. He'd shot up three, maybe
four of the bastards. Killed two that he was sure of.
But then he'd had to cut out. He'd only just made it
over the top of the rimrocks with the bay. God, it had
been close. But that little bay horse was worth his
feed, by God. He was worth gold, every inch of him.
And they'd made it. By sticking with it, they had
made it out. But he'd sworn he would be back. And
he had come back. And by damn, he was going to
get his! And too, he was going to even it!

Only he needed to contact the old man. The bugger had told him he'd be out, had said he'd meet
him.

He needed help. Even the old man could help.
And not only showing him where it all was, but in
handling it. And also he could get him things in
town. Even though he was crazy. Crazy as hell.
Crazy bugger!

What he needed really was a partner. He needed
Tom.

It was afternoon when he had returned again to the
ranch and had seen the spotted pony and the strawberry roan. He knew it wasn't the Lazy Diamond
cattlemen. He didn't know who it was. The law? It
took a good while for him to work his way in close
enough to recognize Gulbenkian; he'd seen him often
enough in Stoneville to know who he was, he'd even
spoken with him now and again. The other he didn't
know. He wasn't wearing a star or anything that
showed him to be a lawman. What were they doing

out here? He got as close as he could, but still couldn't hear them. The question was, did they know—or suspect—something?

It was just as this thought occurred to him that the big man with the broad shoulders stood up and walked toward the spotted horse. Gulbenkian followed, and mounted the strawberry roan.

He still couldn't hear them speaking, so he assumed they were satisfied with whatever they had come to see, and were now leaving.

The big man had turned his spotted horse, and he had thought the two of them were on their way out. But without any warning the big man, reaching for his makings or something in his shirt pocket, suddenly looked down near the horse's front feet. In the next moment he had dismounted, kneeled down to look at something on the ground that had been churned up when the cow pony had started to spook some when the rider mounted. What the hell was he looking at? Whatever it was he didn't show it to Gulbenkian, but slipped it into his pocket. Then he mounted up and the next moment they were gone.

He waited until he was sure they had really left, and then he came out of the trees. All he could see was the earth where the spotted horse's hooves had cut up an area where the grass was soft.

He squatted down and studied the ground. The big man had found something. What?

Sir Cecil Broadhurst lived on a tight schedule. He believed in being punctual; he kept notes on his meetings, which he read over from time to time so that he was always abreast of the flow of his "campaign," as he called it; and he prided himself on the fact that a certain section of his life which was devoted to Cynthia was virtually unknown to other people who took part in other areas of his activity—his business associates, for example. At the same time, believing as he did in secrecy, he had realized early on in his relationship with Cynthia that he needed other avenues of pleasure besides those that she—albeit superbly—offered.

It wasn't easy to avoid the scrutiny of a woman like Cynthia, but Cecil was clever—as clever as he was ruthless. When Cecil Broadhurst wanted something, Cecil Broadhurst got it. It was marvelously simple: desire resulted in attainment. And, to be sure, the spice was most keen when the desire appeared in circumstances that were most difficult of achievement.

Cecil believed that nothing really worth having was easily attained. It was so with the action of the Liverpool Cattle and Sheep Company, and it was so with his design and plan for the "development" of the Willow Creek land up near Red Rock and Handy Mountain. This project wasn't even known to Cynthia. Nor was his latest interest, which went by the name of Lolly.

Lying in bed with her now, in the cabin he'd managed to get for her just beyond the north edge of town, Cecil looked up at the ceiling, which was actually a sod roof, the house being built of logs, and wondered idly at the profits his companion could rake in with her new role as a madam.

With his eyes still on the sod roof he said, "I think you will have to raise your prices, my dear."

"That's going to be a problem," Lolly said, turning onto her side. They were both naked, and had only just partaken of their pleasure together. Cecil had paid her handsomely. Cecil liked it better when he paid. He realized this about himself and understood that what a man paid highly for he was apt to value a lot more than what he got cheaply. He was trying to get this idea across to the girl.

"I don't know that I could get away with that here in Stoneville," Lolly said.

"Then perhaps it would be necessary for you to move to some place like Denver or Laramie," Cecil replied. "However, I repeat that unless you charge higher you won't ever make it as a madam." He turned toward her, his hand dropping onto her belly. "To be a first-class madam, my dear, it is necessary to be absolutely ruthless."

"Ruthless?" she repeated as though it was a word in a foreign language.

"Tough," Cecil explained, enjoying his role of teacher. "Practical. My dear, it is necessary, essential, always to win."

"Huh." She sighed, dropping her hand on top of his as he began to move it over her warm belly.

"You must show no favorites."

"What do you mean?"

"I mean, for example, you must never—never!—do it for nothing."

"But what if you like someone?" she said softly. "What's wrong with that? You know, I like to enjoy it too."

"My dear . . ." He turned his whole body toward her to emphasize his point, while for even more emphasis in the discussion, his member, which was now rigid again, struck her forcefully in the belly, "My dear, a good businessman, a successful man is careful always to go against his own desire for pleasure. Pleasure, my dear is a luxury. Revenge for instance, as the saying goes, is sweet; but it is better to win and live to tell about it."

She had reached down and was fondling his rigidity, running her palm over it, tickling it with her soft fingers.

"But, honey, there just isn't anything better than this, is there?" she whispered, as she took the head of his cock and rubbed it into her wet fur.

"That's not what I'm talking about, my dear." Cecil almost gasped the words.

"Honey, for me this is the best, the only thing there is in the whole world. Isn't it what makes the world go round, huh, baby?"

And now he was on top of her, his member, hard as a pick handle, driving up into her throbbing cunt. She had her heels up on his back, and her hands were on his pumping buttocks. Her tongue was in his ear as she whispered, "Hon, wouldn't you . . . you just give anything for this? Huh?"

And now as they pumped faster and faster, and deeper and higher, he gasped the words, "Oh yes . . . yes . . . yes, yes, yes!"

Elihu Hoskins pushed back the sheets and swung his bare, bony feet to the floor. For a moment he felt dizzy, but he reached for his plug of chewing tobacco to steady himself. He belched faintly, gaining his balance again, and picked up his knife that was on the bedside table. Carefully he cut a slice and carried it to his mouth on the sharp knife blade. And popped it in.

That was better. That was a whole helluva lot better! He paused, his jaws still, having heard something. But it wasn't the woman. He had heard her go out with the boy. It was the moment he'd been waiting for. Still, he remained, collecting his strength as his jaws began to move again on the harsh, familiar tobacco. He yawned suddenly, scratched under each armpit, and blinked away the tears that had come to each eye in the stretching and yawning. He went through himself, taking a moment, checking for pain or stiffness or anything foreign.

He was all right. Well, he would have to move fast but careful. Easy did it, that was the best way. Easy. He stood, pulling the sides and seat of his longhandles, which he wore—like any outdoor man —winter and summer both.

Carefully he took a step. And then another. His back hurt. He could feel the wound moving as he walked. He just had to be careful that it didn't open more and start to bleed. He looked about for a place to spit, then spied the thunder jug under the bed. Handy. By golly, that girl knew how to do things. He liked her, and, in a way, was sorry to leave. Like this. Without saying 'bye and thanks and like that. Well, he'd come by sometime again maybe. She was a good one. Well, why not? The daughter of a man like old Kneecaps. He had known old Kneecaps this good while, and knowed him to be a man for the trail. How the hell he'd ever wound up to be building boxes for folks to die in was more than he could figure.

He sat down on the edge of the bed and pulled his pants on, lifting the wide yellow galluses over each shoulder. Then, careful not to be overtaken with dizziness, he pulled on his boots. He thought of Tip. Tip always used to come and help him get his boots on, licking his hands, wagging his tail. Poor old dog —chewed up by those goddamn wolves up on the Shortwater. Well, he could use a dog now. All he had was Hiram. But what he needed was a horse. He'd never make it out there on foot. He'd have to get a horse, and by golly he'd have to move quicker, on account of the girl would likely be back sooner than a man could think it.

And too, he had promised the man he would meet him. The man was going to help him. He needed him, a younger man. For there was a lot of hard work ahead.

He'd gotten himself ready now, picking up his jacket. He already had his hat on—he'd put it on while he was still in bed, almost without noticing, like it was the most important thing and so taken as something regular, hardly noticed, like a man buckling on his gun.

Elihu didn't pack a handgun. He had an old Henry rifle, or had had it, he reflected as he looked for it in the room. They had taken it, or it had gotten lost. Something. He walked into the front room now but didn't see the Henry. Where the hell was it? Damn! He'd had that rifle ever since, well, a helluva long time. That 16-shot .44 repeater had never failed him; for good reason they'd called it "that damn

Yankee rifle that can be loaded on Sunday and fired all week!"

He was on the point of giving up as he moved through the house looking for it, for he didn't dare linger in case the girl came back, or the boy. But then he saw it. He felt all right then. He really wouldn't have liked taking off without the Henry. Hell, it was as much a part of him as Tip had been. And, by golly, as faithful.

It was late afternoon, he realized as he looked out one of the front windows at the street that led into the town. Good enough. It would soon be dark. And he could use the cover of darkness. The question was how to get hold of something to ride. But maybe Hiram had to be the answer. He was no saddle horse, for sure, but then himself in his present fix was no fancy rider neither.

But where was Hiram? Then he remembered having heard one of them saying—maybe that feller who'd brought him in from where he'd been hit— that the burro was down to the livery. Made sense. Well, he would slip out of the house, hide himself till it was dark enough to get down to the livery without being seen, and locate Hiram.

It was cool on his hands and face when he stepped outside the kitchen door into the backyard. The sun was right at the horizon. They faced each other—he and the sun—as he stopped for a moment once again to check himself. He did feel weak, but he was all right. He was all right long as he took it slow.

He stood now in the backyard chewing thoughtfully on his tobacco, spitting every now and again, scratching himself, and breathing in the clear high air of the Wyoming country.

After a moment he looked up and saw the evening star. And he remembered that time over on the western side of the Absorokas, when he'd been a boy and his dad had shown him how to read sign down by the river breaks. Or was it up on the Musselshell? Hell, now he wasn't sure. But it was somewhere. He knew that, by God. His old man had sure taught him that. How long ago? It didn't matter. What mattered was what was now, not then. And it didn't matter where, on account of everything was right here. And right now. His dad had told him that, too. And so had that old Cheyenne, Lost-His-Horses.

The sun was down now and the chill was stronger. He could feel it in his shoulders. It was good. Sure better than lying in that bed, though that was nice too. Only not for too long.

Elihu bent over a little now and held his thumb against his nostril and blew his nose. Then he did the other side. Then he cut himself another slice of tobacco, and scratched himself, and started in the direction of the livery.

He was looking forward to seeing Hiram. He hoped that Tip was there too. He hadn't seen the dog in a good long while, he knew, but he might be there. He might be with Hiram. It would be good to see him. He'd known Tip longer than he'd known Hiram. Good enough. A man needed a dog. In this country a man with his dog, his burro or horse, and a decent rifle . . . he didn't need anything else.

Then suddenly, he stopped. He had forgotten something. What was it? Tip? Tip was dead. Well, he reckoned he was getting old. No, Tip wouldn't be at the livery. There was only Hiram. Well—good enough.

At Red Rock the men were occupying themselves with cards, dice, horse racing, wrestling, and an occasional fistfight. Big Nose had engaged in battle with both Honus Johnson and Mickey O'Roary, who had already done battle with each other in the basement of McTough's Saloon, and now Big Nose had roundly defeated each one. Big Nose was in a feisty mood. He was still smarting from his handling by John Slocum. No one had ever handled him like that. It had to be a mistake, even though it had happened twice. The man wasn't living who could be that good, handling the likes of himself. And to prove his point, Big Nose had taken on first O'Roary and then Johnson. Yet he was still not satisfied. The two episodes with Slocum still rankled.

The dozen-odd men in his charge noted Hendry's mood. They knew the reason, and they knew very well the result should anyone cross Big Nose. O'Roary and Honus had made the mistake of displeasing their ramrod in some small way, and so had suffered the consequences. O'Roary had a lump on his jaw the size of a fist, while Honus Johnson could hardly walk, having been kicked severely in the crotch at least three times.

Someone had just broken out a harmonica and was working it up when the dry ground began to boom like a great drum, and they saw a pony streaking in with its rider. It was one of the Harrigan brothers, who yanked his sweating horse to a stop right in front of Big Nose, throwing out a sheet of dust, to the annoyance of the group of cardplayers, who received the brunt of it.

"What the hell's the matter with you?" bellowed Big Nose, his fists on his hips like mallets. "You got a snake up yer ass!"

"Wagon coming," said Butch, the words cutting out of him in his excitement. And in fact he was actually out of breath.

"So there's a wagon? You act like the whole United States Cavalry was riding your ass, fer Christ sake!"

Butch grinned. He liked excitement. And he was one of the few who wasn't afraid of Big Nose. "Thought you might like to be ready to welcome himself."

"Himself? Who the hell you talking about?" demanded Big Nose.

"It's that medicine man feller, the one sells snake oil. The one with that cute-looking woman."

"What they doing out here?" somebody asked in a high voice. "They aiming to sell snake oil to us?"

This brought a laugh from the group.

"What about the woman?" Big Nose said. "I seen that wagon in town when that hawker and that old buzzard of a prospector was stripping the greenhorns.

"Feller told me they was looking for Red Rock, Looking for Dicer. So I told 'em to foller me in. I come on ahead fast to tell you." He threw his head in the direction from which he'd ridden so hard.

"You can tell him to come on in," said a voice from beyond the group that had gathered to hear Butch's news.

All turned to see the man who had come out of the log cabin several yards away and had approached without anybody seeing him.

"In fact, send two riders to escort the wagon. You, Google!"

It was Dicer facing them, standing there in his black broadcloth, his white silk shirt, his black wide-brimmed hat, and his black mustache.

The group had stood quietly, and now Big Nose Hendry started to move to carry out the order. But before he could actually say anything, Dicer went on.

"You dumb shitheads! Fer Christ sake, I come out of the cabin and walked right up to you without a one of you assholes noticing! What the hell good are you!"

His eyes were like black bullets as he stared at them. And because his anger was without any visible or audible emotion—he had spoken quietly, icily—it was all the more effective. It was as though a rattlesnake had promised something.

"Get someone out there to bring them in," Dicer said, without looking at Big Nose. "An escort. Two men will be enough. Hurry it!"

Then, turning to Big Nose after the orders had been given, he nodded toward the cabin. "I want to see you."

"Hurry it!" Big Nose shouted after the men, for he felt the need to assert himself in the face of Dicer's backwatering him with his hard way.

Inside the cabin Dicer sat down at a table where he had been having coffee. He did not offer any to Hendry, who remained standing.

"We will be moving out soon," Dicer said.

"The men are getting restless."

"So I see. And they are getting soft. I expect you to keep them up to the mark."

"I whipped a couple their asses just now," Big Nose said. "That put 'em back in line."

"There will be a meeting in here, and I don't want those buggers hooting and hollering out there like a bunch of horny coyotes. You understand?"

"I'll keep 'em quiet."

"Tomorrow I want two riders. Pick your two best men. I'll be doing a little scouting. So I want men who know the country. And I want good horseflesh."

Big Nose Hendry nodded. "This snake oil merchant and his woman, they gonna stay in the cabin here? Or you want something fixed up?"

"There will be four of us staying in the cabin tonight."

"Four!"

"You heard correct. In the morning, the three visitors will be leaving, after I show them around. And then I will be riding out with them and my two riders. You got that."

It was a statement, not a question. And Big Nose did have it.

At that moment they both heard the wagon and accompanying riders coming in and pulling up outside the cabin.

Dicer nodded to the door, and Big Nose stepped quickly to it and and opened it in time to see two men and a woman descending from the canvas-covered wagon with the fancy writing on the side advertising Professor Oldfinger's Absolute Elixir.

Big Nose had only seen one of the three before, but as they walked into the cabin and were met by Dicer, he heard Sir Cecil Broadhurst call the other man Archie. Big Nose thought the woman was beautiful.

9

Slocum of course realized that the raids on the Rocking Box and other herds and on numerous outfits
around Stoneville were the work of intentionally
small war parties so that the Army wouldn't spend
time chasing them. Frustrating from the point of
view of the Army and civilians, but superb tactics for
the "Indians," these forays were becoming intensified. The problem was also intensified by the fact
that the raiders were not actually Indians, but whites
dressed as Indians, using arrows, tomahawks, and
leaving other native articles around the scene. And
while this masquerade was seen through by many, it
also sowed confusion and even fear among the white
families, which was very likely its main purpose. So
Slocum reasoned.

He had ridden back to town with Ulysses Gulbenkian, and after checking that his room at the Jersey
Hotel hadn't been broken into again he had a beer at
McTough's, and a second beer at Harry Skull's. Then
he walked down to the livery and, deciding to give
his spotted pony a rest, rented a hardy black horse

with a white blaze on his forehead. When it was dark enough for cover he saddled the animal and rode out, heading south. When he was a distance away from the town he circled around and headed for Hil Hogan's place. He felt better working alone. It wasn't that Gulbenkian had been a hindrance. It was only that he felt freer to move, to see, to take risks. At the same time he was hoping that his ruse of pretending to find something on the ground when the man in the trees had been watching was going to work.

He camped at the top of a long coulee a couple of hours' ride out of town. For a while he sat on his blanket, which he had thrown by a tall cottonwood, and listened to the night, watching the sky, and trying also to piece together some of the strands that for a while now had seemed to have nothing at all to do with each other.

And yet he didn't push his thoughts, but let them come in and develop, or not, as they wished. One thing was clear, and that was that someone was mighty interested in the section of land that Gulbenkian had identified for him as Hil Hogan's place. He had made quiet inquiries about Hogan when he'd stopped in at McTough's and Harry Skull's places in town after parting with Ulysses. The general feeling was that Hogan was a tough man, not a man to mess with, but he wasn't any killer; that he ran his own outfit, probably with a little "borrowing" here and there, the way any sensible cattleman had always built his herd. By God, the big men had done it often enough. But nobody claimed Hogan to be a mean man. But the "Indians," or maybe the owlhooters at

Red Rock—or both—had fired his place after Hogan had again turned down Cal Bowker's offer for his land. No one was accusing Cal, but it had happened, just like that. And Hil Hogan had shot up a bunch of the attackers who had set the fire, killing two of them, and then he'd hit the trail. Some said he'd gone to Texas, but there had been a rumor that he was still in the country.

Slocum wouldn't have bet against it being Hogan out at his old outfit when he'd spotted the man in the trees and he and Gulbenkian had taken off. In fact, he was counting on it.

Then there was the old man, Elihu Hoskins. What was he doing in the picture? Man looking for gold all his life, and heading for—it was pretty certain—Hogan's place, and getting himself arrowed with a Cheyenne arrowhead. Fake evidence, just like the massacre where he'd found Fidget, and the stampede at Blazer's Crossing.

And where did the Liverpool Cattle and Sheep Company fit in? Obviously, if Cal Bowker and his Lazy Diamond had wanted the Hogan section, then that meant Liverpool wanted it—Cecil Broadhurst and his bunch, whoever they were.

Mixed in with all that was a desire to visit Lolly, whom he hadn't seen in some time. He'd been told that Lolly was in business for herself now, out on the Gold Hill Road, heading south from town. But though he wanted to check her both for information —if she had any—and for physical pleasure, he decided not to take the time. It was important to get back out to Hogan's place. Enough time had elapsed so that Hogan would figure he had gone for good. At any rate, that was what Slocum was planning on.

At the same time he was really looking forward to seeing more of that cute, luscious Annie Hardy with those big, softly shining brown eyes.

"The thing is to keep everything very simple, and that's my point." It was Cecil speaking, and he was speaking to his old and present associate Archie.

They were in Cecil's office in town and had already spent an hour together going over the major points of the campaign. Now they were discussing the letter that had been stolen during the raid on Slocum's hotel room.

"The trouble," Archie said, "is that you can't make head or tail of that letter. It's all smeared. All we get from it is that the writer—whoever the hell that is—is writing somebody named Tom telling him things are great—wherever he is writing from, and we don't even know that—and he should come right out and bring the family. And we can't read the name of the person who signed it. Or even if he's from around this country."

"You said it looked like maybe 'Bill,' and I agree. But I agree mostly to the maybe," Cecil said.

"I need some more coffee," Archie said. "I know I'm supposed to be drinking tea, being English, but I can't stand the stuff."

Cecil got quickly to his feet and walked to the side door of the office and opened it. Putting his head around the door he called out to Cynthia's fine buttocks, which was all he could see of her, as she was bent over picking up her scissors.

"My dear, could you bring a spot of tea, for both Archie and myself?"

She stood up and turned, her face flushed, smiling broadly at him for having caught her in such a compromising position.

"Don't gentlemen usually knock before they enter, Sir Cecil?"

"Maybe gentlemen do, my dear, but I think in the case of entering, it's the wise man who simply does it. And speaking of entering . . ."

"I'll bring the tea, and you get back to business!"

"Later?" he said, cocking an eye at her.

"I think we can 'ave a go. Why not?" And she was gone out the other door for the tea, leaving him with his excitement and his amusement too at her Cockney accent.

In a few moments the two men were settled with their tea, fortified with some brandy, and now again facing their question.

"The point is to keep Liverpool, that is, McIntosh and Georges and Tillson, in the dark about this particular section of land," Cecil was saying. He held up a restraining hand, as he felt Archie was about to speak. "I'm just going over it from the beginning, so we don't miss anything. I have always insisted, as you well know, Archie, that it is in detail that a plan is successful or not."

"I know, I know." Archie waved his hand impatiently and reached for his cup.

"Now listen. I've done all I can to dissuade the boys from wanting to buy the Willow Creek section, Hogan's place. I think I've succeeded. Told 'em it was all rock, poor feed, all that. But of course, mind you, there is actually that part of it that is pretty good grazing." Cecil paused to take a drink of his tea and brandy. "I let them have their say on that, didn't play it down from our part. Then I brought in the idea that we ought to let that lush section go—it's not all that big, I pointed out—since we have all that land around it, which means that without buying that part, Liverpool will control it anyway. They took it, hook, line, and sinker. They don't want it. They are still hot for saving money and cutting down on unnecessary expenses. And get this—they especially liked the idea that turning down that section would make Liverpool look good."

Archie beamed all over. "The Liverpool Company is *not* greedy!"

"We—*we*—Archie, are."

"Of course." Archie shrugged. "Isn't that how we planned it all along?"

"We did. But now it is in action. Dicer and Google and the boys will simply take over the whole section, including Hogan's place, and Liverpool will hand over that special section to Ajax, that is, to us, though of course they will have no idea that it is 'us.'" Archie shifted forward in his chair in his excitement while the two of them warmed to the story as they told it to themselves for maybe the tenth time, the plan that they had been developing for some months.

"They can find out," Archie pointed out.

"By then it will be too late. We'll have cleared the deal."

"I know that. But suppose, well, suppose there's been a mistake. Suppose there isn't anything there?"

"I've thought of that. I sent a surveyor, as I told you," Cecil went on. "And he was very, *very* positive."

"Glory be to God!" And with an absolutely idiotic smile, on his face, Archie Holmes rose and began to dance a jig.

Cecil burst out with a roar of laughter.

After a long moment of hilarity the two quietened.

"Let's be serious now," Cecil said. "We have to take into account the possibility—I say, possibility —of failure."

"Don't you trust the surveyor?"

"I do."

"And that old prospector? He probably knows more about it than a dozen surveyors."

They fell suddenly silent. It all seemed just too good to be true.

"What about Hogan?"

"And what about Slocum?"

Silence claimed them once again.

Then finally Cecil spoke. "It's quite clear what is to be done," he said. "We must get title to that section through our dummy company, Ajax. That's number one." And as was his habit, Cecil began to tick the points off on his fingers. "That is number one."

"Number two," said Archie, imitating him with his fingers. "Number two is for Liverpool to take over the whole section, the grazing plus the rocky section, the whole of it."

"Including our lot," said Cecil, ticking it off on his fingers.

"Including our lot," repeated Archie, doing the

same. "Nobody knows where the lines are drawn except us."

"And then?" Cecil's face began to move into a smile, which slowly widened as he waited for Archie to speak.

"And then, Ajax steps in and asserts its title to that particular section."

Both of them were beaming.

"I think that calls for a drink in celebration," Cecil said.

"I always had confidence in you, Cecil," Archie said warmly.

"So did I," Cecil said as he took two glasses from a nearby shelf and began to pour the brandy.

"We will then have Liverpool by the balls," Archie said.

"They can buy us out."

"Or maybe we'll have enough on hand to buy *them* out," said Archie, and he chortled, making his face long and very British-looking to the delight of his companion.

"Clever," Cecil said. "Damn clever to think of getting the mighty Liverpool Cattle and Sheep Company to do our hard, dirty work for us."

"Well, they can afford to take over that land. They have the men, the guns, the money, everything that's necessary for the enterprise. While we . . ."

"While we have the brains!" Cecil slipped in quickly.

And together they downed their drinks, chuckling with satisfaction at how they were going to use Liverpool to set themselves up with a gold mine.

Cecil poured another round, and for a while they

were silent, each going over the details of the plan to himself, looking for loopholes, the possibility of mistakes, and finally the steps necessary to execute the acquisition of the Hogan property.

"Hogan is an outlaw," Cecil said suddenly, speaking actually to the roof of the cabin.

"So then it shouldn't be difficult to take over."

"Only if he happens to return to this country could there be some trouble." Cecil lowered his glance from the ceiling and now looked at his glass of brandy. "There are rumors that he will return. The other day I had Google send men to take a look round his place. He has, I have heard, an abiding hatred for the Liverpool organization, and myself in particular. Heaven knows why."

"Cecil, how do you see the actual steps to handling those men Slocum and Hogan? Or am I asking a stupid question?" And Archie, half joking, half serious, chuckled as he reached for his drink.

"You are asking a stupid question, Archie."

The big man seemed to be well gone, and probably wouldn't be back. At least not for a while, depending on what he had found. He looked like the kind who would find something, something where another person had overlooked it. And he looked like he could handle that gun he was packing for cross-draw.

Hogan had picketed his bay horse where there was good grazing, and now he broke out a can of peaches and some beef jerky. He built a small fire and boiled coffee. It was enough—not great vittles like he would have liked in town, say, but enough to keep him going. But he did need supplies, and the old man hadn't gotten here.

Hil Hogan sat by the small fire, which was well hidden from any curious eyes unless they were right on top of it, and let it die down. Then he threw his coffee dregs on it and stood up and scattered it with his boot. He sat down again and built a smoke and wondered what had happened to the old prospector.

He had met the old man a while back, just after the trouble with the Lazy Diamond bunch and Bowker and that English sonofabitch. The old prospector had been down by that thin stream working off Willow Creek. He'd surprised the old boy, but he hadn't frightened him any. He could see he was a tough one. Old, and likely crazy as a coot. But by golly the old geezer had been panning, and he had some of that yellow stuff on his britches.

But he hadn't been scared of himself standing there with that Schofield ready to drill him right now. Maybe he was too damn crazy to be scared. Anyway, he'd holstered the Scoff and the old man had given him a mug of coffee that was so strong it was almost chewing stuff.

The short of it was he'd made a deal. What with himself knowing his time was short if he was going to save his skin by getting out of the county, it made sense.

"I'll work this out with you, Elihu," he'd said. "You are on my land here. And if you've really found it, then we'll work out a deal."

"A deal?" the old man had said.

"I could drill you right now and leave you over yonder for the buzzards and coyotes."

"Reckon you could," Elihu said and cut himself a plug of chewing tobacco. "But wish you'd wait and do it tomorrer."

"Tomorrow? Why tomorrow?"

"I mean not today. See tomorrer's my birthday."

"Your birthday!"

"I'll be a hundred, according to my reckoning, and I'd sure like to make it to a hundred. You know, in this country it ain't easy for a man to get to be a hundred years old."

Hogan had laughed at that, but he'd let the old man have his wish. "We could make that deal, like I started to tell you," he'd gone on.

"What deal?"

"I got to get away from here for a while. I need someone to keep an eye on my place."

He had thought Elihu would jump at the offer, but to his astonishment the old man had said, "I'll turn it over."

"What the hell do you mean by that?"

"I'll study it. Man don't want to rush into a thing, you know."

"You'll be here working this," Hogan had said, pointing to the area where Elihu had started his panning. "And we'll go partners on it."

Then the old man had been silent, and had simply gone back to his panning.

Hil Hogan had taken out his makings and was building himself a smoke when suddenly Elihu, without looking up from his work, spoke. "I turned it over an' I'll stick around," he said.

"I'll meet you back here come spring—early,

roundup time," Hogan had said. "That ain't long from now."

"I know when spring is. You got cattle?" The old man squinted at him. And Hogan had been interested because it was the only question he asked.

"Not anymore. The sonsofbitches run 'em off, an' like you probably seen, they burned my place to boot. A week ago. I just made it out of here or they'd of got myself."

Hogan had finished his smoke while the old prospector continued to work. And when he stood up to leave he said, "Just take care nobody sees this here, or you'll never make it to a hundred and one."

Elihu Hoskins had looked up from his work then, from where he was squatting by the creek. But he didn't look at Hogan, he squinted into the distance.

Then he'd said, "Mister, anybody lives to be a hundred in this country has got to be dry back of his ears."

Now, returned to his spread in the early spring, Hil Hogan continued to sit by his dead fire. He rolled himself another smoke. Where the hell was the old man? Had they caught up with him? He had already walked down to the creek where he'd last seen Elihu. There was no sign of him, and it was clear that nobody had been in that area, maybe not even since the time he'd been there himself and spoken with the old prospector.

He didn't think Elihu had talked about his find. The old boy wasn't dumb, but he might have gotten drunk and talked, or he might have gotten touched in the head, like so many crazy prospectors. Damn!

So maybe, maybe he'd have to slip into town and

see what he could pick up. It was risky. Damn risky. Even foolish. But, hell, if something had happened to the old man he could wait here forever. And if the Liverpool gang had gotten hold of him, then it was going to be rough. God, he wished he'd hear from Tom. Well, maybe in town. Maybe there'd be word from Tom in town.

Still one hundred years old, Elihu Hoskins presently was making his way along the trail that would bring him back to Willow Creek and sooner or later his meeting with the man Hogan. It was taking him a long time. Hiram was no sleek cow pony, or even a regular range horse, but he was—Hiram. He was a burro, and he exemplified all the characteristics attributed to those domesticated animals subsumed under the name of mule or donkey. That is to say, Hiram was very much like his master Elihu—stubborn, tough, ingenious in the exercising of his willfulness, and no stranger to guile. In short, the journey was slow, and conducted at Hiram's pace.

At times Elihu rode Hiram, and at other times he led him. The hours passed, and finally Elihu decided to make camp. He was tired. And so he pitched camp in a meadow, right at the edge of it in the protection of aspen and some spruce. He picketed Hiram and unrolled his bedding and slept. He was too tired to eat, though he did give his faithful burro water and grain.

He awakened with the sunlight on his face, dancing through the trees, and he realized he was sweating. He sat up, pulled up his galluses, and built a fire for coffee.

His back hurt him. It had hurt him the day before, but this day it hurt more. But he told himself, a man didn't get to be a hundred in this country without his being tough. So he ignored it. He broke camp, and by mid-morning he was on his way again. But he had to admit he was feeling tired.

It was late that afternoon that he decided to make camp again. He was very tired, and his back hurt him a lot. But he had himself and his Henry, and there was Hiram. He thought of the man Slocum who had helped him, and the girl and the young boy, and old Kneecaps McFadden, wondering how that man had ever gotten such a name; and he thought of Hiram and his dog Tip. Where was Tip? he wondered as he sat under the big cottonwood tree and let his gaze fall all the way to the far horizon.

He didn't hear the men. The next thing he knew they were standing all around him. A big man with a big black beard was pointing a gun at him.

"What you want?" Elihu said, coming more into himself.

"We want you, old man," said the big man with the black beard and the big nose.

"I know you," Elihu said. "You be—"

But he didn't finish what he was going to say, because the man with the big nose suddenly hit him right on the jaw, and Elihu didn't remember anything more after that.

It had been a powerful blow. Big Nose Hendry had had to kneel to deliver it, for the old man was sitting down.

"Did you kill him?" somebody said casually.

"He's breathing," someone else said.

"I didn't hit him hard," Big Nose said. "And by God, you mind it this time, no fucking up like before with that fucking arrer!"

Nobody said anything. For one thing no one felt the remark applied to them. None of them had been engaged in the arrowing of Elihu. That had been arranged by Big Nose, and it was obvious he was only trying to pass the blame, trying to establish a blame on others for the future. But nobody objected. No one dared. Everybody knew full well that Big Nose Hendry could hit a man a whole lot harder than he had just hit the old prospector. And some of them had even been there at the Hoodoo outfit when Big Nose knocked a steer down with his bare fist. Hit him just behind the ear and killed him.

Hil Hogan was thinking of Elihu Hoskins's one hundred years as he was feeling his own sixty, riding the trail back down to Stoneville. He had picked an old game trail most of the way, following within reach of the regular trail down from Willow Creek and the northern country. And he had traveled quickly though with care. He was pretty sure no one knew he was back in the country, and he was hoping to keep it that way. Only now he was going to have to risk it. He'd waited long enough for the old man.

At the same time, he was much satisfied to have found that nobody had discovered the Willow Creek find during his absence. Actually, the chances had been on his side, keeping it secret, for no one around even voiced a hope of the mining coming back to life. The Liverpool bunch and all the small cattlemen were deep into stock growing. He'd even heard talk

of a push on to get the railhead extended to Stoneville to help the cattle business. Good notion, that—
for them. He grinned as he rode toward the town.

Hogan was grinning because in spite of the danger
he was running he was thinking of Lolly. He remembered her talking about wanting to set up as a madam
and run her own girls, and he wondered if she'd thus
retired from active business. He sure hoped not.

As he got closer to the town he wondered again
how he would approach. It wouldn't do just to walk
into McTough's or the Silver Dollar or Skull's place.
It would depend on who was around, of course. No
marshal, he'd heard. That feller Hardy had been
back-shot. He was a good man, Hardy. Hadn't de-
served something like that. But no point in thinking
soft on such matters.

He was wondering too how he would get news of
Tom. But there could be a letter for him, though Tom
had written long ago that he was coming. The trouble
was there was no one to ask without giving himself
away. Except maybe Lolly.

Then suddenly it hit him like a first crack of lightning over a herd of longhorns—that moment of
shock, a split second—before breaking into a stampede. Gulbenkian! Gulbenkian would know something, if anyone would. He had that newspaper and
he hated Bowker's guts. By God, why hadn't he
thought of Gulbenkian before. Hell, he'd known Kit,
Gulbenkian's girlfriend, and her old man who'd been
busted by Bowker's Lazy Diamond men.

Tom Spofford had stood up to them, and paid for
it. But he was a mulehead. He'd refused help from
any neighbor. Well, Spofford was an old-timer. Like

himself. He too had turned down the chance of help. Of course, he hadn't trusted some of them. But then, who could a man trust? Well, he was trusting that old prospector to keep his mouth shut. And he was ready to get to work with him now—now that things had maybe blown over, or at least cooled some, and the Liverpool bunch would leave him be for a spell. For long enough so's he could get some of that gold out of the ground.

10

It hadn't been difficult slipping into town. He'd tied his horse in a back alley, out of the way of any light falling on him. And as a second precaution he'd avoided the main saloons like McTough's and Harry Skull's and had chosen the Five-Shot, a grubby, small saloon on the south end of town. He had never been in the place, but he knew it was one of the lesser establishments, out of the way, and he had a better chance of not being recognized, since he'd always frequented Skull's, the Silver Dollar, or McTough's.

The problem was that Lolly had worked upstairs in Harry Skull's place, and that it wasn't likely they'd know in the Five-Shot if she was still there. That is, without a lot of comment buzzing around.

But Ulysses Gulbenkian wasn't in his office, not at that hour of the night. So it had to be a saloon after all.

Still, he had to take the risk if he wanted to meet her. More and more he was feeling not only the need for a woman but the need for news of what was going on in town and in the surrounding country, and somehow to get news of Tom.

He was lucky. The first person he encountered, the young barkeep at the Five-Shot, knew right off that Lolly had left Harry Skull's and had set up business on her own in a log cabin on the north end of town.

"That gal's sure got something," the barman said. "People ask for her. I never had her myself, but I'm about to see what it's all about. I mean, a woman can draw business like that—a feller like yerself coming in here off the trail and askin' for her, why hell, she's just got to have something real special."

Hil Hogan grinned at that. "I wouldn't know," he said. "I'm a relative."

The bartender suddenly took a hard look at him. But then he immediately caught himself and looked bland at his customer. But Hogan knew he'd been recognized.

He lifted his glass and drained its contents. When he put the glass back down on the bar he said, "Mister, you ever hear of a feller name of Hil Hogan?"

"I don't believe so," the young man almost stammered.

"Then you're lucky. I mind the time I saw Mr. Hogan. Some feller had claimed he knew him. And you know what happened? Huh? You know what happened?"

"Why, no. No, mister, I don't." The young man had picked up the bar rag and was wiping the top of the bar, and he almost knocked over Hogan's glass but saved it in time.

"Why then, I'll tell you. This feller Hogan, he

drew his Colt .44, and he shot that poor sonofabitch right in the guts. Why, that man's guts spilled all over the floor. I mean, it was one helluva mess!"

For another moment he held his eyes on the bartender, and then he turned and walked out of the Five-Shot saloon.

Up at the north end of town, the likely looking place from the description he'd been told was the large log house that apparently had once been an inn.

A young blonde opened the door for him.

"I'm looking for Lolly," he said. "This the right place?"

"It sure is." She was young, with a big bust and large blue eyes. "Who do I tell her is calling?" she now asked in a high voice.

"She'll recognize me," Hogan said. And the girl instantly caught on and said nothing. He put her one grade ahead of the Five-Shot's bartender in intelligence.

At that point Lolly came into the room with a big smile on her face.

"Hi, hon! Long time, huh!" And she held out her hand.

"You're lookin' great, Lol."

"So's yourself, big boy. I missed ya. But you see, I've got my own business now."

"Don't you work yourself?" Hogan asked. His eyes were covering all of her as he spoke, and he could feel not only was she terrific, but she was even better than before. By God it had been a good idea to come to town. But he cautioned himself that he still had to be careful.

"I don't do it for money anymore, hon."

"Great. Then I'll have a free one."

"Sorry, hon. I meant what I said. But look, I've got some great girls. Wait here a minute, I'll get a couple who are free."

"All right," he said. "But I want to talk to you private anyway. I've been away."

She had started to leave, to fetch some of the girls, but his words stopped her.

"I know. And I don't know that it's so good you being here. I mean, for either or us."

She nodded toward a doorway at the far end of the room. "Come on down. I'll talk to you. But only a minute."

"That's all I need," Hogan said as he followed her down the room.

He was just about to follow her through the door when for some reason he looked back. A girl and a customer had just entered the parlor from one of the side rooms. The man had his back to Hogan. There was something odd, something familiar in the man. Hogan knew he had seen him before. He was almost certain he knew him. And he knew that if he knew the man, then it could well be that the man knew him. The man hunched his shoulders suddenly then as he reached for the handle on the front door, and a shock ran through Hogan.

"Come on in," Lolly called from the room she had just entered.

Hogan quickly turned so that his face couldn't be seen by the man leaving the front door.

It wouldn't have served his purpose at all to be recognized by Chick Dicer.

* * *

Riding along after passing Arrow Butte, Slocum watched the country flatten out before him, saw the colors slowly changing on the sage and bunch grass. The color of the water in the creek that he now saw to his right changed too, first clear and light, then murky, for it was mixed with melting snow that had come down from the mountains. To the south he could see the gray color of the sloping country, glinting in some places beneath the blazing late-afternoon sun.

Ahead on his left rose a thin fringe of box elders lining another creek. He followed the dim narrow trail over a sparse hummock and came upon a new view of sweeping green and brown and yellow. Below him a band of pronghorn antelope grazed.

He knew it couldn't go on very much longer. Pretty soon now Elihu or Hogan would make a move —or the Liverpool bunch. Gulbenkian was convinced that Big Nose Hendry was working for Liverpool, that is, for Broadhurst. Slocum was not in disagreement with that. But he knew from bitter experience that no matter how tough Big Nose might be, how able a ramrod of that bunch of gunmen out at Red Rock, he couldn't keep them in check forever. He had felt it when he had studied the canyon through his field glasses, even though he had been a good distance away. Yet, the tension there in the canyon had been quite clear. Sooner or later that force would have to be released. In fact, it would be released whether by plan or by accident.

It was beginning to cool now as he and the black pony dropped down a long draw to a wider creek. The horse picked up his gait, smelling water, and

Slocum decided that the cottonwoods below would be a good spot for a rest, since he knew most of the remaining trail would be in timber, and some rock, and would be tough going.

He let his horse stand in the cool water and drink and rest its legs. He drank himself and filled both canteens—one for himself, one for his pony. The sun had just reached the horizon when he mounted up and they started toward the higher ground which would lead to Hogan's place.

He had not ridden directly toward the Hogan place, but had done some meandering, looking for sign. It was just as the sun was almost gone that he found the place where someone had camped. He dismounted and studied the prints of horses and men, and the prints of a burro. He also found the Henry rifle in the underbrush; he wondered if the old prospector had left that on purpose for anyone who might read what had happened there. Like himself.

It was clear to Slocum what had happened. He didn't stay long at the site, but followed the tracks for a while—long enough so that he knew they were heading toward Red Rock. Then he turned off the trail and pointed the little black horse toward Willow Creek.

It was in the middle of the night that to his utter amazement Sir Cecil Broadhurst awakened with his thoughts racing. This kind of thing never happened with Cecil. He had always been a solid sleeper. But this night he was all at once wide awake and thinking about Hil Hogan and the letter that Big Nose Hendry's men had taken from Slocum's room at the

Jersey Hotel. The letter that he and Archie had been unable to decipher. They had read a few words and had wondered who the writer was, and who the receiver. Until just now—with the naked, mildly snoring Cynthia fast asleep beside him, Cecil suddenly thought of Hil Hogan. Why on earth Hogan? Why? Hil!

He sat straight up in bed, and the woman beside him mumbled but went on sleeping.

It was crazy. Hil! He got up and padded out of the room and into his office. Quickly he struck a match and lighted the lamp, and now he took out the letter and examined it again. Yes, it could be Hil. Why had they assumed Bill? It didn't matter. One's brain often played tricks, and the letter had been so badly smudged.

But then who was Tom? Who had sent the letter? And had it been to Hogan? Well, he was probably pushing it. And did it really matter? The plan was set. Except that if it was Hogan, then it might mean that someone was coming out, maybe a family person, and maybe someone who now knew that the land there had something else on it besides grass.

He sat down and reached down to the small cupboard and brought out the bottle. Ah, that was better. He had to watch it. That was important. It was not good to let himself get tight because of the excitement and the gamble. He'd certainly been under a strain with all the hard work of planning, keeping the boys in line, especially Dicer, and convincing first Archie and then the others at Liverpool. Because it was fantastic, such a coincidence. If it was so. If it was really so! Yet he didn't need it really. It was by the way. What he needed was to keep straight thoughts. For it had been his adage and his rule for all these years that the shortest distance between two thoughts, and between a thought and an action, was a straight line. And then, he would always add, except sometimes. He smiled now, thinking of that.

Presently he returned to bed without waking Cynthia, who, still asleep, snuggled up to him. But he was too much in his thoughts to feel any special excitement, as usually he would have.

He lay on his back now, with his eyes open in the dark, seeing only what was in his thoughts. In the morning he was going to have to talk with Dicer. Dicer had sent word in ahead. They'd found the old prospector out on the trail someplace and had brought him in to Red Rock. But they'd gotten nothing out of him of any importance because he had passed out.

So he would see Dicer tomorrow, that is, actually, in just a few hours. Yes! He closed his eyes, relaxing. It was getting to be time for action. And as always at such moments, he knew he would do it on his own, without consulting even Archie. For that was how he worked best. By some kind of inside knowing. In the past it had always worked like that; and on the other side, when he talked too much to Archie or anyone else, when he planned too much, it didn't work.

He turned over then and his erection stabbed into his bedmate, who responded instantly by opening her legs. He slid his hand down and found her soaking wet.

"What a delightful response, my dear," he whispered.

"Why did you wait so long?" she said. "I've been going crazy."

Cecil thought he had never felt so excited as she turned toward him. In a moment he asked her, "How would you like it, my dear?"

Cynthia mumbled something he could barely hear. Her mouth was full of his erect organ; and Sir Cecil didn't repeat his question.

"Who is Tom?"

Slocum came out with the question at the same moment that he stepped out of the line of trees facing the ruin of the Hogan ranch.

Hil Hogan had just ridden in as the sun was bearing down well into the afternoon. He looked over at the tall, broad-shouldered man with the raven-black hair and sharp green eyes who was holding no gun on him but was just standing there loose and easy.

"Reckon you are Slocum," he said drawing rein.

Slocum nodded.

Hil Hogan threw his leg forward over the pommel of his stock saddle and dismounted. Real limber for his age, Slocum noted.

"Missed you last time you was here," Hogan said. "You and that newspaper feller. I been wondering if you found what you was looking for that time. Or maybe you was just diddling me standing over there in the trees, figuring to worry something."

"What I was looking for I just asked you, Hogan," Slocum said. "Who is Tom?"

"How'd you come by that name, Slocum?"

"Fair enough," Slocum said with a slow smile. And he told Hogan about the letter and the massacre when he'd found the boy.

"You're saying the boy had the letter with him?"

"In his pocket. Only he didn't maybe even know it. He actually could have just picked it up somewhere. It doesn't mean it was his, or related to him. Like I say, he was deaf and dumb. At least at first; then he got his hearing. But he still doesn't speak."

"What's he look like?"

"Small, about seven, maybe eight. Lots of wheat-colored hair. Blue eyes."

"Skandihoovian-like, from the way you tell it."

Slocum nodded.

"You got the letter?"

"Somebody stole it out of my room at the Jersey Hotel."

"Shit." Hil Hogan squinted at the sun, spat, shifted his weight, and then stood, swing-hipped, with his hands plunged one in each hip pocket.

"Funny world, ain't it?" he said. "The way things happen. That could be Tom Hogan's boy."

"Your brother?"

Hogan nodded. "I wrote him a good while back, wanting him to come out with Ethel and the boy. But I've never seen Tom's boy. Tom moved back East about eight years ago, after—after things got kind of busted up. I mean the law got on our ass. I did a stretch in Folsom, and Tom went east and married. I never met his wife."

"You free now?" Slocum asked.

"I'm free now. Done my time, and I got papers to prove it."

"How come there's a dodger on you then?"

"Stockmen's Association, courtesy of that Liverpool bunch. It's a fake. They want this place." He spat suddenly, sighed, and looked at an eagle soaring through the high sky. "I wrote Tom hoping he could help me. I got myself domesticated, too. But she— Mary—up and got the consumption. Nothing the doc could do. So I bin batching ever since."

Slocum had listened carefully. He remembered having heard of the Hogan brothers now. A good while back they'd been the bane of more than one or two banks, plus Wells Fargo. Then, as with most of their professsion—nothing. Boot Hill or the pen.

"I got a notion that could of bin Tom in that rubout. And Ethel and maybe the boy."

"What was the boy's name?" Slocum asked.

"Dunno. You call him something?"

"Fidget."

A wide grin appeared on the old bandit's face. "Good name that. On account of he don't, huh?"

Slocum grinned and said nothing.

They had led their horses toward the shade of the trees, and each ground-hitched his animal and let him graze at will.

"You got the makings for some arbuckle?" Slocum said.

"You build us a fire and I'll be right with it," Hogan said.

Shortly they had their coffee in tin mugs and were squatting, but not too close to the fire for it was still a warm day.

"Where do you fit into all this here?" Hogan asked. "I mean, you bin out here at least a couple times and maybe more. What is it you're after?"

"Started out by looking for the boy's father or mother," Slocum said. "Then I got hooked up with Gulbenkian. You know him?"

"Everybody knows Gulbenkian. Man's lucky he ain't already had his ass shot off by Dicer and Big Nose and them boys."

"Dicer? Is that Chick Dicer?"

Hogan nodded. "He's whipsawing Broadhurst's gang with Big Nose Google. You know Big Nose?"

"Our paths have crossed," Slocum said with a grin.

"He's a tough boy."

"I do believe he's a little less tough than he was."

Hogan gave a big laugh at that.

Then Slocum said, "What about Elihu Hoskins?"

"It's him I bin waiting for," Hogan said. And he told Slocum how he had asked Elihu to watch his outfit while he hid out for a while from the Liverpool bunch. "See, they want this section of land more'n a bull wants a cow in springtime. I mean it! The sons-ofbitches!"

"I've seen some of that yellow stuff around," Slocum said. "Could it be that they're after?"

"Where'd you see it?" Hogan asked carefully.

"On Elihu Hoskins," Slocum said. "And I was always good at arithmetic. I know two and two makes four."

"Well . . ." Hogan let out a heavy sigh. "I guess there's no sense in trying to hold out on you. I think you've got the situation pretty well sized up."

"By now Cecil Broadhurst and his bunch know there's gold here, wouldn't you say?"

"I'd say just about everybody in the country knows it, along with all his relatives." Hil Hogan's expression was as sour as a lemon.

Slocum couldn't repress a smile. Then he turned serious. "I didn't know Dicer was here," he said.

"I saw the sonofabitch down at Lolly's new sporting house."

"Did he see you? Does he know you?"

"He knows me, and if he didn't actually see me, he will have heard by now." He ran his hand over his face. "I'm laying odds that that's why he's here. He figures he owes me."

They fell silent for a moment or so, while the horses cropped at the short grass under the trees, their bits clinking, the leather saddles creaking. Now and again one or the other would shake his head at a deer fly, or stomp with his hoof, or even shake his head with the bridle and bit jangling. It was hot.

"I know they got hold of Elihu," Slocum said. "I followed his trail on my way up here. If he's still alive he'll be at Red Rock."

"Then they'll likely as hell be here quicker'n soon," Hogan said. "The old boy won't be able to hold out against Dicer. I mean, maybe he can—he sure is tough and ornery as a bear with a bee up his ass—but he's old."

"He's old enough to fool them," Slocum said. "But they don't have to get him to say anything. They'll figure it out, if they haven't already."

They were again silent, and then Hogan said, "Well, it ain't the first time."

"What ain't the first time?"

"It ain't the first time I bin up shit creek with nothing," Hogan said.

"Well, maybe we can hope it also ain't the last," Slocum said. "Have you got papers to this place? Title?"

"Sure have." And then seeing the thoughtful look on Slocum's face he asked, "Why? Why do you want to know that for?"

"Suppose something happened to you. Who would get this place?"

"A relative, I guess. If I had one."

"I see."

Then they were silent again, two men of the trail, neither one too close to the law nor too far. That depended on how a man looked at things. For Slocum, it had always been a question of how you were inside, not just what was written on a paper. A man's word, not his signing something. But men dealt with paper more and more nowadays, it seemed.

The coffee was good, and Hogan kept it hot on the small fire. Now the sun took more distance as it got closer to the western horizon, and there was an extra warmth in the air, almost like a last reminder that the day was going to end and soon it would be cooler.

Slocum had been watching the horses, and now he saw the black lift its head suddenly with its ears forward and up. Then Hogan's bay nickered.

"Somebody coming," Slocum said.

In a trice they were on their feet and had moved into the trees with their guns drawn.

A long moment passed while they waited. And then they both saw him. He was down the slope beyond where the cabin had been before it was fired.

Slocum and Hil Hogan watched from the cover of the trees while Elihu Hoskins walked toward the fire that was still heating their pot of coffee.

"You will therefore have a free rein—up to a point," Cecil was saying to the dark man with the slicked head of black hair, the black mustache, the very white shirt and black coat and California trousers.

"It's a good moment," Dicer said. "You have nothing to worry about."

"I was not, and certainly am presently *not* worrying," said Cecil Broadhurst testily. "I am only warning you to be cautious. I know you have a—well, a thing about this man Slocum, though I don't believe you've ever met him. And of course, about Hogan. So I am cautioning you not to compromise the company or, worse, myself." He cleared his throat, looking directly into those black eyes. "You understand me. No one else is to be hurt. That is important."

"I do."

"Then remember one thing clearly. You will be paid only according to your understanding."

Sir Cecil walked to his desk and sat down.

Dicer walked to the door of the office. He opened it, and with his hand on the knob he turned, throwing his hard eyes at the man at the desk. "I have been waiting a long time for this," he said. "Those two are dead."

Sir Cecil continued to sit at his desk. He appeared to be reading something, and he didn't look up as Dicer left the room.

After a moment there was a knock on the door and Archie entered.

"All done?" he asked, seating himself in one of the available chairs.

"All set." Cecil tossed his pen onto the desk and looked at Archibald Holmes. "I don't like it, but I see the need to move fast."

"Because of Fitzwilliam sending a marshal."

"That's still a rumor, but where there's smoke there's . . . the other, or course." Cecil sat back in his chair. "No, it's time. I just hope that damn fool Dicer doesn't get it into his head to mess around with that kid and Hardy's widow."

"But why would he do that?"

"To draw out Slocum. He knows, he found out that Slocum found the boy at the massacre site and brought him to Mrs. Hardy. You know what Gulben-kian would spread all over his goddamn newspaper if anything—I mean, anything—were to happen to that young boy."

"Or the woman."

"Dicer is a killer."

"Isn't that why you hired him?" Archie said, bland as a spring morning.

Cecil looked at his longtime business associate. He stood up, pushing back his chair. He squared his shoulders. "Yes," he said. "Yes."

11

Slocum hadn't felt too good about leaving Elihu out at the ranch, and so he'd made him ride double, first with himself on the black horse with the white blaze on his forehead, and then with Hogan on his bay.

The message had been simple and brooked no delay. Dicer had given the instructions to Elihu Hoskins personally.

He would meet John Slocum and Hil Hogan in town the following day. Good enough; but it was in the next part of the message that Slocum felt something cold running through him. And Hil Hogan felt the same movement no less in his guts. Dicer gave his word that neither Annie Hardy nor the young boy in her charge would he harmed in any way. As both men knew, the threat couldn't have been put more cleverly.

In any case, it was clear to Slocum why things were coming to a head. First of all, Broadhurst and Dicer could see that himself and Hogan were both at hand, plus the rumor that a new marshal would be sent from Fort Fitzwilliam, and plus too the building feistiness of the Red Rock gang. He knew it was going to blow soon, and so he wasn't surprised. But the mention of Annie Hardy and Fidget had been unexpected.

Despite the extra rider, they got to the outskirts of town in reasonable time. Elihu was holding his end up. He had ridden part-time with Slocum and part with Hogan, gripping his old Henry rifle which Slocum had picked up from the site where he'd read sign of the Red Rock boys taking the old prospector.

It was dark when they reached the town's outskirts, and Slocum drew rein near a low benchland.

"I'll go in first," he said. "I'm going to try to locate Gulbenkian. They'll sure enough be watching him, and also the Hardy house."

"You know where Gulbenkian stays? I couldn't find him the other night," Hogan said.

"He stays with his girl Kit. He told me where. Maybe they're not watching the place. I'll take a chance. You two split up. I'll be back in maybe an hour, maybe longer. We'll camp yonder, away from that creek. Near those trees. Elihu, you get some rest."

The old man, who had hardly spoken a word all the way in, snorted and popped a fresh chew into his snappy old jaws. "Rest, huh! This here's the time to stay awake, not rest. You rest now, mister, it'll end up bein' permanent!"

"Hogan, how are you fixed for ammo?"

"Not too good, my friend."

"We'll go along that back street behind Mogus's General Store. He's got what we want."

"That's what I know," the old outlaw said. "I have

borrowed from Mr. Mogus before. How you fixed?"

"You can pick me up a couple of boxes of .44-40 for the Winchester."

"Good there isn't a moon."

"I could use me a drink," Elihu said.

"You stay away from them saloons," Hogan said. "After this is over we'll all get drunk as hell."

"Likely drunk with lead whiskey the way it looks like," the old man said, mumbling the words as he started after his two companions.

It was past midnight by the time Slocum had found and talked with Gulbenkian and Doc Entwhistle and finally Kneecaps McFadden. His plan was to meet them, along with Elihu, in the early morning. It hadn't been easy, for the town was up late, as always, but it seemed to be especially awake this night. There was—and Slocum could feel it like a touch—an ominous atmosphere in Stoneville that night. It was as though everyone knew there was to be some kind of showdown the next day. Yet Slocum knew too that the majority of the citizens, while maybe feeling this charged atmosphere, would have no idea at all what it was about. It was like that in the western towns, he knew. The drama of kill or be killed was always there, like the scenery or the drink at one of the saloons. Nobody ever questioned such things. It was ritual, accepted in varying degrees throughout the populace starting with the participants and traveling on out to the merest spectator or purveyor of news.

He had not gone to see Annie or Fidget, for he knew the house would be watched. But he had gone

to Kneecaps' cabin and talked with him, telling him
what to do the next morning.

The last person he spoke to that night was Hil
Hogan. "I want you to sign over your outfit, Hogan.
That fair enough?"

"I have already done so," Hogan said. "I went to
see Entwhistle just after you left him. And he's got
the paper. I also got the ammo from Mogus's store."

"Now we're ready," Slocum said. "Get some
sleep."

"I'd like to see the boy," Hogan said. "If he is
Tom's boy that makes me his uncle. And if he's not,
I'm still an uncle for Tom's son, anyway."

"Maybe after. I've been by the house. They've
got it sewed tight."

"How you figuring on turning this thing, Slocum?" Hogan said then. "I'm backing your hand all
the way, but shit man, there's just two of us and who
knows how many of them!"

"I hope that's just what you're going to see tomorrow morning, Two of us, and the whole of them."

Slocum lay down in his bedroll, about a mile out
of town, with Hogan and old Elihu not too far away.
He slept lightly. At one point he found his thoughts
on Annie Hardy, but he stopped them. Later, he told
himself. There would be time for that later.

All at once it was the dawn. It slipped into the sky in
the same way it had always done, without any argu-
ment, even discussion. The morning was simply
there. It came on its own terms and in its own time.

Ulysses Gulbenkian was watching the sky from
the window of the cafe where he had come for

breakfast, foregoing this morning, as he occasionally did, breakfast with Kit. This day he had told her to stay inside, or at least stay off Main Street. And now he sat in the Ruby Cafe, looking out at the morning, thinking, It doesn't care what happens down here. When we're all dead and gone—maybe even by this afternoon—morning will come tomorrow, and the day after, and the day after.

He was feeling strange. Poetical, he told himself. Strangely too, he felt good. He knew he had no control over anything. What was going to happen was going to happen. It gave him something he had always wanted and never really attained. A sense of freedom.

When he went out into the street the strange feeling was still with him. Somehow, he could think of no other word to tell it to himself; somehow everything—himself too—felt infinitely more real.

Old Elihu Hoskins walked out into Main Street carrying his Henry rifle and a few rounds of spare ammo in his pockets. He didn't stay in the street, but crossed to the sunny side, stepping up onto the wooden boardwalk. He would thus have the sun helping him rather than being in his eyes. He had his orders from Slocum to watch the rooflines.

Kneecaps McFadden, whose eyes were as strong as the rest of him, took the side where the sun was on him, but he knew he could handle that. What the hell, he'd told Slocum, eighty-eight wasn't as old as a hundred, like that old fart on the other side of the street. He too could surely watch the rooflines. Doc Entwhistle and Ulysses Gulbenkian would be watching the alleys.

This drawing together of the drama was already under way by the time Sir Cecil Broadhurst stepped out of his house. He had had a good breakfast, and he anticipated a congenial supper that night when everything had been settled. He walked briskly to the gig waiting for him. He stepped in, muttering a good-morning to the driver.

The next thing Cecil knew, there was something very hard poking into his ribs.

"Shut your mouth and do what I tell you. In case you don't know me, mister, it's Hil Hogan, and one funny sound or move outta you and I'll blow your balls off!"

Cecil Broadhurst had virtually stopped breathing. It didn't matter, for there was nothing more to say as the horse and gig moved slowly along the street until the driver found a shady spot near McTough's Saloon and across from Kneecaps McFadden's undertaking parlor, and then he drew rein.

"What the hell do you think you're doing?" Sir Cecil demanded.

"I am guarding your life, Broadhurst. I'm not going to allow anybody to kill you but me."

The street meanwhile had acquired some more guns, and these were in the hands of the members of the Red Rock banditti. Big Nose Hendry, his huge snout and great black beard covered with his huge red bandanna, strode across the street seeing that everything was in order.

"We're keeping the peace," he bellowed, his voice greatly muffled by the bandanna, which did nothing whatever to disguise him; but then, as Ulysses Gulbenkian had once pointed out in print, perhaps Big

Nose saw the bandanna not as a disguise but as costume.

The street was quiet. Horses had been taken into back streets, so that the hitching racks were empty.

Suddenly a young child, a little girl, broke out of a doorway and ran into the street. She was very young, her legs were short, and she fell. Her mother came racing after her and grabbed her up and sped to safety.

"Our men are here to see there is fair play!" Big Nose suddenly bellowed.

At that point a spotted horse came slowly along the street. John Slocum rode straight in the saddle, as he always did. He rode all the way down the street until he came to the last frame house, which was painted white and had flowers outside. He had seen the gunmen, and he had also seen the citizens who were watching the street through various windows of the stores, saloons, and other buildings.

Slocum drew rein, dismounted, and hitched his spotted horse to the rail outside the white house. His arrival and his destination were watched by everyone with mounting surprise. He walked up to the door, opened it, and entered.

The house, he knew, was already empty, for he had sent Elbows to pick up his daughter and Fidget before dawn. But there was something there in the house that he needed. And he had already asked her for it.

When he came out into the street he was wearing the badge of a United States marshal. He didn't mount his horse but walked back down the way he had just ridden on the spotted pony.

A murmur ran through the crowd.

And then it came. "Who the hell does he think he is? Where'd you get that tin, Slocum!"

He had come as far as about the middle of the town now, and he stopped.

"This here isn't my badge," Slocum said in a loud, carrying voice. "It belongs to a marshal who was shot in the back here in Stoneville. So I'm borrowing his tin just for a little while until we get something settled here. Meanwhile, I'm waiting for Dicer. And meanwhile too, Mr. Cecil Broadhurst is under arrest in that gig there. My deputy has orders to shoot him dead if any of you monkeys on those roofs or in those alleys thinks he's going to drygulch me. You got that!" He waited a beat, then another. And then, "Throw down your guns now and come down off those roofs and out of the alleys. I mean right now!"

Nobody argued it. The guns fell. The men came down to the street.

But where was Dicer?

Then he saw him. Dicer had stepped out from the alley next to the bank and was walking toward him. His arms were down at his sides, and he was holding his two six-guns by the barrels.

"All right, Mr. Marshal, sir. We are law-abiding citizens. And here are my guns." And to everyone's astonishment, the man in the black suit with the obsidian eyes and the low-brimmed Stetson hat threw his guns on the ground.

"No hideout!" Dicer said as he slowly removed his coat, pulled his white shirttails out, and patted his body to show he had no concealed weapons. "I'm clean." Dicer laughed. "You want me to take my boots off, Marshal?"

Slocum didn't answer. He could smell the trap being set—he knew it through the tingling along the back of his neck.

"I want Big Nose right here in my sight," he said, hard.

Dicer had reached up to remove his hat. "Got nothing in my hat neither, Slocum." He was holding the hat in his left hand, and held his right well away from his side.

"It's hotter'n Hades today!" somebody called out from somewhere behind Slocum.

In that same second Slocum knew it wasn't.

He dropped just as the mirrored sunlight coming from an upstairs window all but blinded him, while Big Nose tossed the hideout he'd had in his shirt to Dicer.

Slocum, momentarily blinded, lost his man, but he had taken the chance in the split second that Dicer would shoot at his head or upper body. And he was on the street as Dicer's shot went over him, at the same time that he had drawn his gun and fired twice as he lay on his back in the street.

His first bullet hit Dicer in the neck and passed up through his head. His second hit Big Nose Hendry Google in his guts. Neither of his two adversaries died slowly. Big Nose, trying to use his second hideout, hadn't even pulled the trigger.

When Slocum walked up to the gig where Hil Hogan was guarding Cecil Broadhurst, the prisoner said, "So they got you to be a lawman after all, Slocum."

"Just helping out till the man gets here, mister. You got anything else?"

"No."

"Just remember one thing. When you or any of those people you work with at Liverpool start getting itchy again, just think of Dicer and Big Nose. Fact, I think you might want to take a little trip out of the country for a while. Because there are people about who might take a notion to get mad at you."

As he was walking toward the spotted horse with Hogan beside him, the former outlaw said, "I want to go see the boy, Slocum."

"Good enough."

"I got a strong notion he's Tom's boy, and I'd like—"

"I think he is too," Slocum said, cutting in.

They had reached the spotted horse, and now Slocum picked up the reins in his left hand and, reaching up with the same hand, grabbed some of the long mane to help pull himself up.

"I see you get on like an Indian," Hogan said.

"I bin told I got Cherokee in me."

Hogan was grinning as Slocum looked down at him from the saddle.

"I'll tell you one thing, Slocum—I'm sure as hell glad you weren't the law when me and Tom were night riding."

"Well, I'm not now," Slocum said with a laugh, and he reached up and unpinned the star and slipped it into his shirt pocket.

When he saw her he said, "I want you."

"I know."

"I want you to know that I—"

"I know."

"Is Fidget around?"

"He's with Dad. He's staying there the night. Part of his growing up."

They were in the parlor and it was already night. She was only a few feet away from him, in the chair, but he could feel her as though he was holding her in his arms.

The next moment he was holding her.

"Annie . . ."

"You don't have to say. I know you're not a man who stays in one place for very long. That's all right with me."

He had held her hand as they walked into her bedroom and shut the door. And then he was kissing her. Her lips were soft, totally giving as he pressed his mouth gently to hers.

"Oh, you're so gentle," she whispered.

"I don't know if what I feel for you will always stay gentle," he said, softly.

"Nor I for you," she said suddenly, and bit his lip, but not at all hard; teasing.

Slowly they undressed each other, until they were totally naked and his erection was stabbing into her thighs, her crotch, and as she bent over to open the bed, into her high, firm breasts.

Then their naked bodies were entwined as she straddled his big manhood and rode on it, rubbing her hairy wetness, as she whimpered with pleasure at each stroke. He cupped her breasts with his hands, feeling their firmness. Then, bending, he took one nipple in his mouth and sucked, while she drove her tongue into his ear, and with her hand now played with his balls.

"Oh, I've been wanting you so," she cried in his ear, and gently bit the lobe, then again ran her tongue inside his mouth while he sucked it; and then she took his tongue. At the same time their bodies began their rhythm as she grabbed his now huge organ and directed it into her eager cunt. And together they rode, in the most perfect rhythm. Never had Slocum felt so joyful.

Now they worked faster, faster, and their bodies pumped in perfect unison until at last they held and held and finally could no longer bear it and let the exquisite explosion suffuse them.

"Oh my God, my God," she cried. "Your thing. It's so marvelously huge! My God, you're splitting me! Oh, don't stop! Don't stop—ever, ever, ever." And they came and came . . .

They lay limp, sealed to each other, and even slept for a little while.

In a short time their passion collected again, and this time she licked him into an ecstasy he could never have imagined, sucking his organ until he thought he would go crazy. Then, reversing herself, she sat her bush in his face while they sucked each other into another total oblivion.

He stayed the night, and they both slept for a while, then awakened and did it again.

In the morning—after sleeping like a baby—he awakened to find her nipple in his face, and she held her breast as for a baby while he sucked and chewed, and with her other hand she stroked his manhood until it was covered with shining come. Then she rode on top of him; then took him from behind while he pumped her deliciously, holding each of her breasts in his eager hands while she reached back to squeeze his balls. And then, at almost the point of coming, as if by some unknown signal, they both turned to embrace each other, he on top, with her legs spread wide for him, and he held her tight as they came in the same exquisite instant.

Later, with the sun well up, they had coffee in the kitchen.

After a while Slocum said, "When will Fidget be back?"

"I'm to go and get him anytime. Dad's letting him help in his carpenter shop."

"I see."

A long moment fell between them, and he could feel it widening.

Then Annie said, "You're leaving."

He nodded.

"I wish you could stay."

"Would you believe me if I said I wished so too?"

"Yes. I do believe you. I'll not forget you, John Slocum."

"Nor I."

"What about Fidget?"

"He's got an uncle now."

"But maybe he's lost someone else."

"I'll be with him in a different way," Slocum said.

She held him with her brown eyes then, as though her whole body was listening to what he'd said. "I understand. Yes, I understand."

Shortly, he rose and walked to the door, and

turned. They stood there, smiling into each other's eyes.

"Do you ride?" he said suddenly.

For a second she looked surprised. "Of course."

"Thought we might have a picnic. I don't have to be anywhere special for the next day or so."

She was smiling, her happiness bursting out of every part of her. Slocum was laughing as he watched her joy.

"Shall we take Fidget with us?" she said. "Or do we want to be alone?"

"I'd say we want to be alone, but let's take him with us."

"We'll have tonight," she said.

"And tomorrow night." He reached over and squeezed her arm. "You know, I ain't catchin' the stage, or a boat or a railroad train. That spotted horse out there waiting can just wait as long as we feel like it."

She had already reached under a table and brought out a hamper.

"'Course, we better find out if Fidget can go with us," Slocum said. "He might be doing something with his uncle."

"Oh, I forgot."

"We can see. Let's go over to your dad's house and see."

And as they started down the street toward Knee-caps McFadden's house Annie said, "Do you think Fidget will ever speak?"

"Sure. Why not?"

"But . . . why doesn't he speak now?"

"Dunno. Maybe he doesn't have anything to say."

They were within sight of Kneecaps' carpenter shop now, and they could see the boy carrying some tools through the door. He didn't see them.

They had both stopped in the street for a moment.

And then Annie said, "But . . . when do you think he will speak? Ever?"

Slocum turned to her, admiring the profile of her nose. "Why, I reckon he'll speak when he takes a notion to. When does anybody?"

JAKE LOGAN
TODAY'S HOTTEST ACTION
WESTERN!

___SIXGUN LAW #113	0-425-10850-3/$2.95
___SLOCUM AND THE ARIZONA KIDNAPPERS #114	0-425-10889-9/$2.95
___SLOCUM AND THE HANGING TREE #115	0-425-10935-6/$2.95
___SLOCUM AND THE ABILENE SWINDLE #116	0-425-10984-4/$2.95
___BLOOD AT THE CROSSING #117	0-425-11233-0/$2.95
___SLOCUM AND THE BUFFALO HUNTERS #118	0-425-11056-7/$2.95
___SLOCUM AND THE PREACHER'S DAUGHTER #119	0-425-11194-6/$2.95
___SLOCUM AND THE GUNFIGHTER'S RETURN #120	0-425-11265-9/$2.95
___THE RAWHIDE BREED #121	0-425-11314-0/$2.95
___GOLD FEVER #122	0-425-11398-1/$2.95
___DEATH TRAP #123	0-425-11541-0/$2.95
___SLOCUM AND THE CROOKED JUDGE #124	0-425-11460-0/$2.95
___SLOCUM AND THE TONG WARRIORS #125	0-425-11589-5/$2.95
___SLOCUM AND THE OUTLAW'S TRAIL #126	0-425-11618-2/$2.95
___SLOW DEATH #127	0-425-11649-2/$2.95
___SLOCUM AND THE PLAINS MASSACRE #128	0-425-11693-X/$2.95
___SLOCUM AND THE IDAHO BREAKOUT #129 (On sale Sept. '89)	0-425-11748-0/$2.95
___STALKER'S MOON (On sale Oct. '89) #130	0-425-11785-5/$2.95

Check book(s). Fill out coupon. Send to:

BERKLEY PUBLISHING GROUP
390 Murray Hill Pkwy., Dept. B
East Rutherford, NJ 07073

NAME_____

ADDRESS_____

CITY_____

STATE_____ZIP_____

PLEASE ALLOW 6 WEEKS FOR DELIVERY.
PRICES ARE SUBJECT TO CHANGE
WITHOUT NOTICE.

POSTAGE AND HANDLING:
$1.00 for one book, 25¢ for each additional. Do not exceed $3.50.

BOOK TOTAL	$ ____
POSTAGE & HANDLING	$ ____
APPLICABLE SALES TAX (CA, NJ, NY, PA)	$ ____
TOTAL AMOUNT DUE	$ ____

PAYABLE IN US FUNDS.
(No cash orders accepted.)

202